I would invite you to play, but I'm way across an ocean and at the very end of the lane, up four flights of stairs and under the roof where you can barely stand up when you reach the third grade! But I have the perfect plan. We'll each write a story and collect them in a book, and there we will meet whenever we feel like getting away and spending the day together.

FOR EVERY STAMP
YOU WILL FIND
A STORY.

AUSTRALIA

AUSTRIA

BELIZE

CHINA

CRIMEA

DENMARK

ENGLAND

FRANCE

GEORGIA

INDIA

INGUSHETIA

ISLE OF UNST

JAPAN

MAURITANIA

MOZAMBIQUE

RUSSIA

PERU

RWANDA

SCOTLAND

SOUTH AFRICA

TURKEY

UNITED STATES

WALES

SPACE SHUTTLE COLUMBIA

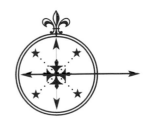

Compiled by
Jeannie Ferber & Priscilla Harper

——

Edited by
Margaret Robinson Millar

——

Artists
Ayingiliye Apollinarie
Michael Chase
Valerie Schurer Christle
Peter Ferber
Dirzhaya Zanaderzhda

——

Printed by
Accura
So. Barre, Vermont

Six Inches to England

A special collection
of international children's stories

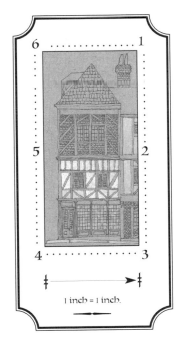

1 inch = 1 inch.

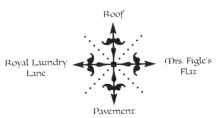

Andover Green Book Publishers

NH

We tried not to lose the world.

OUR HOPE IN PUBLISHING THIS BOOK
IS TO GIVE CHILDREN AN OPPORTUNITY TO DISCOVER THE BEST OF OUR
WORLD ∽ ITS GREAT BEAUTY AND DIVERSITY. YOU'LL FIND MANY WON-
DERFUL PHRASES AND EXPRESSIONS IN THESE STORIES THAT HAVE NOT
BEEN AMERICANIZED IN TRANSLATION. IN SOME CASES, WE'VE KEPT
REGIONAL SPELLINGS OF FAMILIAR WORDS TO GIVE CHILDREN AN OPPOR-
TUNITY TO SEE HOW DIFFERENCES IN LANGUAGE, AS IN LIFE, DO NOT
MAKE ONE WAY BETTER THAN ANOTHER, BUT MAKE OUR WORLD
MORE "COLOURFUL".

Andover Green Book Publishers
Gilman's Corner
Alton, NH 03809-9716

ISBN 1-885934-07-6

C

By Way of the Mountain

To the Peaceable Kingdom

The Journey Home

Contributing artists:

Ayingiliye Apollinarie, p. 115
Michael Chase, p. 1
Valerie Schurer Christle, pp. 19, 40, 160
Peter Ferber, pp. 18, 80, 84, 128, 142, 150
Dirzhaya Zanaderzhda, front cover and remaining artwork

Six Inches to England

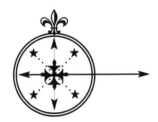

Journey I

BY WAY OF THE MOUNTAIN

On your first journey you must travel by way of the Mountain. From the Mountain you can see all the countries and peoples of the world. It is up to you to discover the name of the Mountain and where to find it.

Journey I

MICHAEL CHASE

Mountaintop map in morning light

One noble act = 500 miles

*High in the mountains
you can still see the towers of our ancestors.*

THE COURTYARD AND THE FENCE

by a man named Zakre

Grandfather Tausi was very old then, and I was the only boy allowed into his room to play on his big, brightly colored carpet. It was a thick, warm carpet—the kind you are always trying hard to dig your toes into. In the center of it there was a small pattern. It was surrounded by another, different pattern. And around that was still another pattern. Each one got bigger and bigger, and brighter and brighter, and more and more beautiful.

My grandfather was a very wise man. I knew it even as a small boy. But I am not saying it just because he was my grandfather, or because he loved me. Everyone said so. He lived in the land of my ancestors, a land called Ingushetia. High in the mountains you can still see the tower of my ancestors. No one is living in our tower now. I have heard, though, that sometimes it is used by shepherds for shelter.

Ingushetia is a small republic that lies in the Caucasus Mountains of southern Russia.

Long ago these towers were used to protect our land. And now I can hear you asking, "Why were your ancestors living in towers for fighting?" The answer is because our land is so beautiful. There are mountains whose rocky peaks turn to gold at noon, and then purple when the sun sets at night. The valleys are always as soft and thick as if it just rained. In the summer there are fields filled with rye and wheat, and fields of tall, tender grasses where children play hide-and-seek. And everywhere there are small, chattering rivers and streams—so many that it has never been possible to give them all names. But for all this beauty we have had to pay a price. All our history has been a story of fighting for our small, beautiful land.

In one thing my grandfather was absolutely different from everyone else. It was not his wisdom. There were other wise men. It was not his bravery. There were other brave men. What made my grandfather different, was that he was always staying on the side of truth. That is how he was described. He was a just man. This reputation he wore like a warm, well-made coat all his life.

When my grandfather was very old he told me a story. This story lives in my heart as if he told me only this morning.

One day while my grandfather was sitting in his room, he heard his son (my uncle) arguing with a Russian neighbor who was putting up a new fence. My grandfather did not understand Russian. He was very old even at that time, with a beautiful, white beard. My grandfather went to his oldest son and asked him, "What are you arguing so loudly about with our neighbor?"

His son replied that their Russian neighbor had moved his fence one-half meter into my grandfather's courtyard.

Then my grandfather said something very quietly, so quietly that his son and the Russian could hardly hear him, and so they had to stop their arguing and listen.

"Say to our neighbor," my grandfather ordered his son, "Do not move your fence one-half meter inside my courtyard. Move it one whole meter!"

5

After that my uncle said it to the Russian who was standing and staring at my grandfather with his long, white beard without understanding him (because my grandfather was speaking in the Ingush language). Do you know what the Russian did? He moved his fence one whole meter into *his own* courtyard! My uncle could hardly believe his eyes!

When my grandfather told me this story, I understood that he wanted me to remember it always. From that day I understood that the example he had given his son was more important than a half-meter of land.

And now you know it, too.

Of all the republics in the Russian Federation, Ingushetia is by far the poorest. Yet, during a time of war in neighboring Chechnya, it was tiny Ingushetia that gave food and shelter to hundreds of thousands of refugees.

When you are deep in the rainforest of the
Amazon Basin, there are not enough words in
any language to describe green. It is more than
a color; it is life. Each texture, each smell and
sound, each shape and variety of leaf and feather,
fish or furry animal—everything, everywhere growing,
creeping, crawling, swimming—glories in just being alive.
     And in this place where the nights are as long as
the days, a place where it is always warm, and
a place where it rains almost every day, there lives a
family: Caspiuma, his wife, and twelve sons. Their
home is in la selva—or the jungle of Peru. For some
people, the word "jungle" calls up exotic images, distant
and dangerous. Yet for the people who actually live in
the rainforest, it is home and provider.
     This story was told to me by Julio, the ninth son
of Caspiuma, whose name means Green Tree. He
was our guide in the Amazon, and he told this story
on Christmas Day 1990 as we paused in a clearing
in the rainforest.

CASPIUMA'S SECRET

A story of the Peruvian rainforest as retold
by Rachel Crandell

Caspiuma was my father. Each day he would go into the forest with his blowgun to hunt for food to feed us. But one day he could find nothing for the cooking pot. No monkeys, no birds, no sloth, no peccary! What could he do? We would all be hungry.

My father was worried so he began to pray. Then, strangely, through the palms and tangle of *lianas* he saw his best friend who was motioning him to follow. Surprised, my father, Caspiuma, called to him, "What are you doing here so deep in the forest?"

The distant figure answered, "I will lead you to a secret place where there is much game. Take only what you need, only one or two animals, and you will always have enough. And don't tell anyone where it is."

His friend started off through the forest and my father followed. But

Peru lies on the north western coast of South America.

sloth: a very slow-moving, toothless animal with three toes, about the size of a small dog.

peccary: a wild pig.

lianas: woody vines.

More than half of all the world's plant and animal species are found in the rainforests, yet they constitute only 5% of the earth's land surface.

he could never catch up, even when he ran! His friend seemed to glide through the forest faster and faster. Tired and breathless, Caspiuma was glad when his friend finally came to a stop. Without a word the figure vanished and my father realized he was standing in a place teeming with the sounds and signs of birds and wildlife. With his blowgun he shot only one animal for our family's cooking pot.

Many times my father, Caspiuma, returned to that place when he could find no other food for us. He remembered the words that had been spoken to him in the forest, "Take only what you need." Sometimes he shared with another family that was hungry, but he never told anyone—except us— where the secret place was.

When others in the village asked my father, Caspiuma, how he always had enough to feed his family, he told them only that he went to a place far away. But whenever he went, it somehow seemed very near, and not to take any time at all to get there.

My father, Caspiuma, was always grateful to God and we always kept that secret—and always remembered, "Take only what you need."

*   *   *

When Julio grew up, he went to the city of Iquitos to go to college. He says he is not superstitious like most people who live in la selva. Julio's education teaches him to demand facts for proof. But when he told us this story, he smiled and said he could never explain with "facts" how his father could always find food when no one else could.

8

The world's rainforests are over 140 million years old. The highest layer, or canopy, has been called "the undiscovered continent" of our world.

The Monkey Poem

9

by Bronwyn Anne Harper
Age 5

A monkey sat on a poem
    He was trying to find a home
He swung from tree to tree
    Then said, "Ah, I'd rather be free!"

*The decision was made to send donkeys loaded
with that year's harvest to Ferlo, guided by the shepherds.*

He who is led by his stomach will always
be led into a hole.

WOLOF PROVERB

MORLAM'S BONE

An old tale from Mauritania as retold by Khady Diop
Translated by Molly Lipscomb

In many villages for many years the fields had been ravaged by plagues worse than had ever been known in the memory of the oldest wise man that could be found. The plagues in Lamene had gone on so long that no man under twenty had ever smelled a pot of cooking meat. But finally the plagues ended, and even Lamene began to recover. That year the rains were abundant, the ground generous, and the crickets absent.

As a result, the decision was made to send donkeys loaded with that year's harvests of millet, peanuts, and corn to Ferlo where the Hal Pulaar tribes passed through with their huge herds of animals. The Hal Pulaar were vegetarian. They mixed their couscous and rice with milk only: fresh milk, sour milk, curdled milk, or yogurt.

Mauritania lies in the northwestern part of Africa.

Couscous is a North African dish of steamed semolina. Semolina is often used to make pasta (like macaroni or spaghetti) and is usually served with meat.

For three moons the donkeys journeyed, guided to Ferlo by the shepherds, the strongest of the young men in Lamene. They had received an order to return with a beautiful seven-year-old bull to be eaten in celebration of the end of the famine. The bull was to be shared by all the families of the village. The best parts were to be given to the oldest men, but everyone would get something—even if nothing more than the smell of meat on the fire. The day the donkeys left with their masters, Morlam decided which part of the bull he wanted.

Finally, the young men returned leading a huge bull whose huge horns shone brightly in the setting sun. From his neck, as massive as the trunk of a baobab tree, to his tail which swept the ground, the great bull was truly magnificent. While risking being chastised, Morlam nonetheless immediately claimed the piece he wanted and then quickly returned home to his wife, Awa, to tell her *exactly* how it was he wanted it to be cooked: gently, slowly, and carefully.

Awa carefully put the bone in the pot and then bent conscientiously over the fire, determined to cook the precious bone as perfectly as Morlam had told her. In the meantime Morlam stretched out comfortably on his bed of branches and pine cones. Soon the aroma of the roasting meat was filling the house of Morlam.

ॐ

In Lamene everyone was very pious and no one ever missed going to the mosque for the seven daily prayers, and so Moussa was very surprised when

12

The word "bone" is used the way the term "ribs" is used in the West. Here "bone" means a side of beef.

Many of the people of Africa are Muslim— or adherents of the religion called Islam. The word "Muslim" in Arabic means "one who surrenders to God."

he had not seen Morlam, his best friend and bloodbrother, at the mid-morning prayer—the prayer of *Yor-Yor*.

You see, the friendship between Moussa and Morlam was stronger than brotherly love and more demanding than fatherly love. Moussa, having mixed his blood with the blood of Morlam at the age of twelve, was forever bound to Morlam. All his life he had sung with him the same songs and all his life he had eaten from the same bowls as him—whether it was delicious vegetables or dry insects.

13

"Morlam won't eat that bone all by himself, he won't eat it without me!" Moussa said to himself, hurrying towards Morlam's house and calling out to him on his way. "Morlam, it's me! It's me, Moussa—more than your brother—your *bok-mbar*, your blood brother! Open the door!"

Having heard the commotion, Morlam called out to his wife, "Where is the bone?"

"The bone is in the pot," she replied.

"Is it softening?"

Awa stood up, uncovered the pot, and poked at the bone. "Yes, it is softening."

"Put the cover back on, stir up the fire, and bolt and lock the door!" ordered her husband stretching himself once again on his pine cone mat trying to forget about Moussa.

Moussa shouted his cordial and joyful salutations through the windows and the door while Morlam grimaced in silence. "One cannot close his door on the nose of a friend," he thought reluctantly, and so Moussa was let in and stretched himself out next to Morlam.

Soon Moussa was carrying on a conversation all by himself, not noticing that Morlam could no longer hear the birds singing or the leaves gently rustling in the trees. Moussa talked about the countryside, then about friends, and then about other friends, and, of course, about all the special times he and Morlam had had when they were young . . . which conveniently led to his reminding Morlam of the obligations they had to each other as blood brothers. Morlam grunted to be polite.

The friends' feet were already in the sun now as the shade in the courtyard shrank. Morlam made a sign to his wife. As she leaned close to him, he whispered in her ear, "Where is the bone?"

"It's in the pot."

"Is it softening?"

Awa went to the pot, poked at the bone, and told her husband, "Yes, it is softening."

The sun had now reached its highest point and the *Imam* was calling out the noon prayer of *Tesbar*. Morlam and Moussa made their absolutions and prayed to their guardian angels demanding pardon from God and forgiveness for their sins, and then returned home to the cooking pot. Still another prayer time passed, and yet another, and finally the time had come for prayer of the *Izan* as the sun began to set. As soon as Morlam had prayed his last prayers, he asked his wife, "Where is the bone?"

"It is in the pot."

"Is it softening?"

Awa uncovered the pot, poked the bone, and whispered to her husband so Moussa would not hear, "Yes, it is softening."

14

Imam: The word means "leader" or "exemplar", and refers to the head of the Muslim community who leads the prayer services.

"Moussa does not want to leave!" whispered Morlam back and feeling very annoyed with his bloodbrother. "I'm going to tell him I'm sick!"

Suddenly Morlam began to breathe laboriously and shiver like milk that's about to boil. Moussa quickly helped him to his bed, for as a bloodbrother Morlam's troubles were felt equally by Moussa. Morlam groaned, shivered, tossed, and turned until the middle of the night. Motioning Awa to come to him Morlam faintly asked her, "Where is the bone?"

"It is in the pot."

"Is it softening?"

"It is softening."

"Awa, I'm going to pretend to die and then Moussa will have to leave!" Having said this, he pretended to die. His wife, screaming and crying, said to Moussa, "Moussa! Your best friend and bloodbrother is dead! Go tell the *marabout* and the people of the village."

"Never," said Moussa! "Never will I abandon this man who is more than my brother to me, nor will I leave you. When the sun rises in the morning the women will pass by on their way to the wells. They can take care of telling the village."

When the ground became cold, and the rooster began to crow, and the sun began to rise from its rest, the women passed in front of Morlam's home and Moussa told them of his death. Such news, of course, spread through Lamene like a whirlwind and soon Seingne, the *marabout*, and his followers were descending on Morlam's house. Awa leaned down close to her husband and whispered, "Morlam, things are becoming too serious! The whole village has come to our house to prepare you for burial!"

15

marabout: a member of an ascetic Muslim order in North Africa residing in ribats, or monasteries.

"Where is Moussa?" asked Morlam in barely a breath.

"He is there."

"Where is the bone?"

"It is in the pot."

"Is it softening?"

"It is softening."

16

"Let them prepare me for burial!" whispered Morlam. "Then Moussa will certainly leave!"

As Seingne, the *marabout*, went to wrap Morlam in a white cloth, Awa said, "Seingne, my husband asked me to recite over his body a prayer that he taught me so that God would have pity on him." The *marabout* and his followers politely stood back while Awa leaned over Morlam and whispered in his ear, "Morlam! Get up! They're going to wrap you up in the funeral cloth and bury you if you keep pretending to be dead!"

"Where is the bone?" asked Morlam.

"It is in the pot."

"Is it softening?"

"It is softening."

"And Moussa, where is he?"

"He is still there."

"Let them set me in the ground then. Then Moussa will finally leave."

The first sand was already covering Morlam when Awa again asked to say her prayers to her husband. "Morlam you have gone too far! Get up!"

"Where is the bone?" asked Morlam from under his sand-covered grave wrappings.

"It is in the pot."

"Is it softening?"

"It is softening."

"Where is Moussa?"

"He is still there."

"Then let me be covered in the grave."

17

Morlam had not yet finished explaining himself to his guardian angel when he was finally covered with sand. He tried to make the angel understand: "Listen, I'm not *really* dead! It's just a bone that brought me here!"

After Morlam was buried, Seingne, the *marabout*, solemnly declared Moussa, as the bloodbrother and best friend of Morlam, to be Awa's husband. So Moussa became master of the house and the fire, and of the bone of poor Morlam.

PETER FERBER

Had she loved the umbrella too much?

THE BLUE UMBRELLA

by Ruskin Bond

"**Neelu! Neelu!**" cried Binya. She scrambled barefoot over the rocks, ran over the short summer grass, up and over the brow of the hill, all the time calling, "Neelu, Neelu!"

Neelu (Blue) was the name of the blue-grey cow. The other cow, which was white, was called *Gori*, meaning Fair One. They were fond of wandering off on their own, down to the stream or into the pine forest, and sometimes they came back by themselves and sometimes they stayed away—almost deliberately, it seemed to Binya.

If the cows didn't come home at the right time, Binya would be sent to fetch them. Sometimes her brother Bijju went with her, but these days he was preparing for his exams and didn't have time to help with the cows.

Binya liked being on her own, and sometimes she allowed the cows to lead her into some distant valley, and then they would all be late coming home. The cows preferred having Binya with them, because she let them wander. But Bijju pulled them by their tails if they went too far.

Binya belonged to the mountains, to this part of the Himalayas known as Garhwal. Dark forests and lonely hilltops held no terrors for her. It was only when she was in the market-town, jostled by the crowds in the bazaar, that she felt rather nervous and lost. The town, five miles from the village, was also a pleasure resort for tourists from all over India.

20

Binya was probably ten. She may have been nine or even eleven, she couldn't be sure as no one in the village kept birthdays; but her mother told her she'd been born during a winter when the snow had come up to the windows, and that was just over ten years ago, wasn't it? Two years later her father had died; but his passing had made no difference to their way of life. They had three tiny terraced fields on the side of the mountain, and they grew potatoes, onions, ginger, beans, mustard and maize: not enough to sell in the town, but enough to live on.

Like most mountain girls, Binya was quite sturdy, fair of skin, with pink cheeks and dark eyes and her black hair tied in a pigtail. She wore pretty glass bangles on her wrists, and a necklace of glass beads. From the necklace hung a leopard's claw. Binya always wore it. Bijju had one, too, only his was attached to a string.

Binya had stopped calling for Neelu; she heard the cow-bells tinkling, and she knew the cows hadn't gone far. Singing to herself, she walked over fallen pine needles into the forest glade on the spur of the hill. She heard voices, laughter, the clatter of plates and cups; and stepping through the trees, she came upon a party of picnickers.

They were holiday makers from the plains. The women were dressed in bright saris, the men wore light summer shirts, and the children had pretty new clothes. Binya, standing in the shadows between the trees, went unnoticed; and for some time she watched the picnickers, admiring their clothes, listening to their unfamiliar accents, and gazing rather hungrily at the sight of all their food. And then her gaze came to rest on a bright blue umbrella—a frilly thing for women—which lay open on the grass beside its owner.

21

Now Binya had seen umbrellas before, and her mother had a big black umbrella which nobody used any more because the field rats had eaten holes in it, but this was the first time Binya had seen such a small, dainty, colourful umbrella; and she fell in love with it. The umbrella was like a flower, a great blue flower that had sprung up on the dry brown hillside.

She moved forward a few paces to see the umbrella better. As she came out of the shadows into the sunlight, the picnickers saw her.

"Hello, look who's here!" exclaimed the older of the two women. "A little village girl!"

"Isn't she pretty?" said the other. "But how torn and dirty her clothes are!" It did not seem to bother them that Binya could hear and understand everything they said about her.

"They're very poor in the hills," said one of the men.

"Then let's give her something to eat." And the older woman beckoned to Binya to come closer.

Hesitantly, Binya approached the group. Normally she would have fled, but the attraction was the pretty blue umbrella. It had cast a spell over her, drawing her forward almost against her will.

"What's that on her neck?" asked the younger woman.

"A necklace of sorts."

"It's a pendant—see, there's a claw hanging from it!"

"It's a tiger's claw," said the man beside her. (He'd never seen a tiger's claw.) "A lucky charm. These people wear them to keep away evil spirits." He looked to Binya for confirmation, but Binya said nothing.

"Oh, I want one too!" said the woman, who was obviously his wife.

"You can't get them in shops."

"Buy hers, then. Give her two or three rupees, she's sure to need the money."

The man, looking slightly embarrassed but anxious to please his young wife, produced a two rupee note and offered it to Binya, indicating that he wanted the pendant in exchange. Binya put her hand to the necklace, half afraid that the excited woman would snatch it away from her. Solemnly she shook her head. The man then showed her a five rupee note, but again Binya shook her head.

"How silly she is!" exclaimed the young woman.

"It may not be hers to sell," replied the man. "But I'll try again." He waved his hand towards the picnic things scattered about on the grass. "How much do you want—what can we give you?"

Without any hesitation Binya pointed to the umbrella.

"My umbrella!" cried the young woman. "She wants my umbrella. What cheek!"

"Well, you want her pendant, don't you?"

"That's different."

"Is it?"

The man and his wife were beginning to quarrel with each other.

"I'll ask her to go away," said the older woman. "We're making such fools of ourselves."

"But I *want* the pendant!" cried the other petulantly. And then, on an impulse, she picked up the umbrella and held it out to Binya.

23

Binya removed her necklace and held it out to the young woman who immediately placed it round her own neck. Then Binya took the umbrella and held it up. It did not look so small in her hands; in fact, it was just the right size.

She had forgotten about the picnickers, who were busy examining the pendant. She turned the blue umbrella this way and that; looked through the bright blue silk at the pulsating sun—and then, still keeping it open, turned and disappeared into the forest glade.

Binya seldom closed the blue umbrella. Even when she had it in the house, she left it lying open in a corner of the room. Sometimes Bijju snapped it shut, complaining that it got in the way. She would open it again a little later. It wasn't beautiful when it was closed.

Whenever Binya went out—whether it was to graze the cows, or fetch water from the spring, or carry milk to the little tea shop on the Tehri road, she took the umbrella with her. That patch of sky blue silk could always be seen on the hillside.

Old Ram Bharosa (*Ram the Trustworthy*) kept the tea shop on the Tehri road. It was a dusty, unmetalled road. Once a day the Tehri bus stopped near his shop and passengers got down to sip hot tea or drink a glass of curds. He kept a few bottles of Coca-cola too; but as there was no ice, the bottles got hot in the sun and so were seldom opened. He also kept sweets and toffees, and when Binya or Bijju had a few coins to spare they would spend them at the shop. It was only a mile from the village.

Ram Bharosa was astonished to see Binya's blue umbrella.

"What have you there, Binya?" he asked.

Binya gave the umbrella a twirl and smiled at Ram Bharosa. She was always ready with her smile, and would willingly have lent it to anyone who was feeling unhappy.

"That's a *lady's* umbrella," said Ram Bharosa. "That's for *Mem-Sahibs*. Where did you get it?"

"Someone gave it to me—for my necklace."

"You exchanged it for your lucky claw!"

Binya nodded.

"But what do you need it for? The sun isn't hot enough—and it isn't meant for the rain. It's just a pretty thing for rich ladies to play with!"

Binya nodded and smiled again. Ram Bharosa was right; it was just a beautiful plaything. And that was exactly why she loved it.

"I have an idea," said the shopkeeper. "It's no use to you, that umbrella. Why not sell it to me? I'll give you five rupees for it."

"It's worth fifteen," said Binya.

"Well, then, I'll give you ten."

24

Binya laughed and shook her head.

"Twelve rupees?" said Ram Bharosa, but without much hope.

Binya placed a five paise coin on the counter. "I came for a toffee."

Ram Bharosa pulled at his drooping whiskers, gave Binya a wry look, and then placed a toffee in the palm of her hand. He watched Binya as she walked away along the dusty road. The blue umbrella held him fascinated, and he stared after it until it was out of sight.

The villagers used this road to go to the market town. Some used the bus; a few rode on mules; most people walked. Today, everyone on the road turned their heads to stare at the girl with the bright blue umbrella.

Binya sat down in the shade of a pine tree. The umbrella, still open, lay beside her. She cradled her head in her arms, and presently dozed off. It was that kind of day, sleepily warm and summery.

And while she slept, a wind sprang up. It came quietly, swishing gently through the trees, humming softly. Then it was joined by other random gusts, bustling over the tops of the mountains. The trees shook their heads and came to life. The wind fanned Binya's cheeks. The umbrella stirred on the grass.

The wind grew stronger, picking up dead leaves and sending them spinning and swirling through the air. It got into the umbrella and began to drag it over the grass. Suddenly it lifted the umbrella and carried it about six feet from the sleeping girl. The sound woke Binya.

She was on her feet immediately, and then she was leaping down the steep slope. Just as she was within reach of the umbrella, the wind picked it up again and carried it further downhill.

Binya set off in pursuit. The wind was in a wicked, playful mood. It would leave the umbrella alone for a few moments; but as soon as Binya came near, it would pick up the umbrella again and send it bouncing, floating, and dancing away from her.

The hill grew steeper. Binya knew that after twenty yards it would fall away in a precipice. She ran faster. And the wind ran with her, ahead of her, and the blue umbrella stayed up with the wind. A fresh gust picked it up and carried it to the very edge of the cliff. There it balanced for a few seconds—before toppling over, out of sight.

Binya ran to the edge of the cliff. Going down on her hands and knees, she peered down the cliff-face. About a hundred feet below, a small stream rushed between great boulders. Hardly anything grew on the cliff face— just a few stunted bushes and, half way down, a wild cherry tree growing crookedly out of the rocks and hanging across the chasm. The umbrella had stuck in the cherry tree.

Binya didn't hesitate. She may have been timid with strangers, but she was at home on a hillside. She stuck her bare leg over the edge of the cliff and began climbing down. She kept her face to the hillside, feeling her way with her feet, only changing her handhold when she knew her feet were secure. Sometimes she held on to the thorny bilberry bushes, but she did not trust the other plants, which came away very easily.

Loose stones rattled down the cliff. Once on their way, the stones did not stop until they reached the bottom of the hill; and they took other stones with them, so that there was soon a cascade of stones, and Binya had to be very careful not to start a landslide.

As agile as a mountain goat, she did not take more than five minutes to reach the crooked cherry tree. But the most difficult task remained. She had to crawl along the trunk of the tree, which stood out at right angles from the cliff. Only by doing this could she reach the trapped umbrella.

Binya felt no fear when climbing trees. She was proud of the fact that she could climb them as well as Bijju. Gripping the rough cherry bark with her toes and using her knees as leverage, she crawled along the trunk of the projecting tree until she was almost within reach of the umbrella. She noticed with dismay that the blue cloth was torn in a couple of places.

She looked down; and it was only then she felt afraid. She was right over the chasm, balanced precariously about eighty feet above the boulder-strewn stream. Looking down, she felt dizzy. Her hands shook, and the tree shook too. If she slipped, there was only one direction in which she could fall—down into the depths of that dark and shadowy ravine.

There was only one thing to do—concentrate on the patch of blue just a couple of feet away from her. She did not look down or up, but straight ahead; and willing herself forward, she managed to reach the umbrella.

She could not crawl back with it in her hands. So, after dislodging it from the forked branch in which it had stuck, she let it fall, still open, into the ravine below. Cushioned by the wind, the umbrella floated serenely downwards, landing in a thicket of nettles. Binya crawled back along the trunk of the cherry tree. Twenty minutes later she emerged from the nettle clump, her precious umbrella held aloft. She had nettle stings all over her legs, but she was hardly aware of the smarting. She was as immune to nettles as Bijju was to bees.

✳

Bijju was on his way home from school. It was two o'clock and he hadn't eaten since six in the morning. Fortunately, the Kingora bushes (the bilberries) were in fruit, and already Bijju's lips were stained purple with the juice of the wild, sour fruit.

He didn't have any money to spend at Ram Bharosa's shop today, but he stopped there anyway, to look at the sweets in their glass jars.

"And what will you have today?" asked Ram Bharosa.

"No money," said Bijju.

"You can pay me later."

Bijju shook his head. Some of his friends had taken sweets on credit, and at the end of the month they had found they'd eaten more sweets than they could possibly pay for! As a result, they'd had to hand over to Ram Bharosa some of their most treasured possessions—such as a curved knife for cutting grass, a small hand-axe, a jar for pickles, or a pair of earrings—and these had become the shopkeeper's possessions and were kept by him or sold in his shop.

Ram Bharosa had set his heart on having Binya's blue umbrella, and so naturally he was anxious to give credit to either of the children; but so far neither had fallen into the trap.

Bijju moved on, his mouth full of Kingora berries. Half way home, he saw Binya with the cows. It was evening, but Binya still had the umbrella open. The two small rents had been stitched up by her mother.

Bijju gave his sister a handful of berries. She gave him the umbrella while she ate the berries. "You can have the umbrella until we get home," she said. It was her way of rewarding Bijju for bringing her the wild fruit.

Calling "Neelu! Gori!" Binya and Bijju set out for home, followed at some distance by the cows. It was dark before they reached the village, but Bijju still had the umbrella open.

Most of the people in the village were a little envious of Binya's blue umbrella. No one else had ever possessed one like it. The schoolmaster's wife thought it was quite wrong for a poor cultivator's daughter to have such a fine umbrella while she had to make do with an ordinary black one. Her husband offered to have their old umbrella dyed blue; she gave him a scornful look and loved him a little less than before. The Pujari, who looked after the temple, announced that he would buy a multicoloured umbrella the next time he was in the town. A few days later he returned, looking annoyed and grumbling that they weren't available except in Delhi. Most people consoled themselves by saying that Binya's pretty umbrella wouldn't keep out the rain, if it rained heavily; that it would shrivel in the sun, if the sun was fierce; that it would collapse in a wind, if the wind was strong; that it would attract lightning, if lightning fell near it; and that it would prove unlucky, if there was any ill luck going about. Secretly, everyone admired it.

Unlike the adults, the children didn't have to pretend. They were full of praise for the umbrella. It was so light, so pretty, so bright a blue! And it was just the right size for Binya. They knew that if they said nice things about the umbrella, Binya would smile and give it to them to hold for a little while—just a very little while.

Soon it was the time of the monsoon. Big black clouds kept piling up, and thunder rolled over the hills. Binya sat on the hillside all afternoon, waiting for the rain. As soon as the first big drop of rain came down she raised the umbrella over her head. More drops, big ones, came pattering down. She could see them through the umbrella silk as they broke against the cloth. And then there was a cloudburst—like standing under a water-fall. The umbrella wasn't really a *rain umbrella*, but it held up bravely. Rods of rain fell in a curtain of shivered glass.

30

Everywhere on the hillside people were scurrying for shelter. Some made for a charcoal burner's hut; others for a mule shed, or Ram Bharosa's shop. Binya was the only one who didn't run. This was what she'd been waiting for—rain on her umbrella—and she wasn't in a hurry to go home. She didn't mind getting her feet wet—and the cows didn't mind getting wet, either.

Presently she found Bijju sheltering in a cave. He would have enjoyed getting wet, but he had his school books with him and he couldn't afford to let them get spoilt. When he saw Binya, he came out of the cave and shared the umbrella. He was a head taller than his sister, so he had to hold the umbrella while she held his books. The cows had been left far behind.

"Neelu, Gori!" called Binya and Bijju.

When their mother saw them sauntering home through the driving rain, she called out, "Binya! Bijju! Hurry up and bring the cows in! What are you doing out there in the rain?"

"Just testing the umbrella," said Bijju.

✳

First the summer sun, and now the endless rain, meant that the umbrella was beginning to fade a little. From a bright blue it had changed to a light blue. But it was still a pretty thing, and tougher than it looked—and Ram Bharosa still desired it. He did not want to sell it; he wanted to own it. He was probably the richest man in the area—so why shouldn't he have a blue umbrella? Not a day passed without his getting a glimpse of Binya and the umbrella; and the more he saw it, the more he wanted it.

The schools closed during the monsoon, but this didn't mean that Bijju could sit home doing nothing. Neelu and Gori were providing more milk than was required at home, so Binya's mother was able to sell a kilo of milk every day: half a kilo to the schoolmaster, and half a kilo (at reduced rate) to the temple Pujari. Bijju had to deliver the milk every morning.

Ram Bharosa had asked Bijju to work in his shop during the holidays, but Bijju didn't have time; he had to help his mother with the ploughing and the transplanting of the rice seedlings. So Ram Bharosa employed a boy from the next village, a boy called Rajaram. He did all the washing-up and ran various errands. He went to the same school as Bijju, but the two boys were not friends.

One day as Binya passed the shop twirling her blue umbrella, Rajaram noticed that his employer gave a deep sigh and began muttering to himself.

"What's the matter, Babuji?" asked the boy.

"Oh, nothing," said Ram Bharosa. "It's just a sickness that has come upon me, and it's all due to that girl Binya and her wretched umbrella."

"Why, what has she done to you?"

"Refused to sell me her umbrella! There's pride for you. And I offered her ten rupees."

"Perhaps, if you gave her twelve . . ."

"But it isn't new any longer. It isn't worth eight rupees now. All the same, I'd like to have it."

"You wouldn't make a profit on it," said Rajaram.

"It's not the profit I'm after, wretch! It's the thing itself. It's the beauty of it!"

"And what would you do with it, Babuji? You don't visit anyone— you're seldom out of your shop. Of what use would it be to you?"

"Of what use is a poppy in a cornfield? Of what use is a rainbow? Of what use are you, numbskull? Wretch! I, too, have a soul. I want that umbrella, because—because I want its beauty to be mine!"

Rajaram put the kettle on to boil and began dusting the counter, all the time muttering, "I'm as useful as an umbrella," and then, after a short period of intense thought said, "What will you give me, Babuji, if I get the umbrella for you?"

"What do you mean?" asked the old man.

"You know what I mean. What will you give me?"

"You mean to steal it, don't you, you wretch? What a delightful child you are! I'm glad you're not my son or my enemy. But look, everyone will know it has been stolen and then how will I be able to show off with it?"

"You will have to gaze upon it in secret," said Rajaram with a chuckle. "Or take it into Tehri and have it coloured red! That's your problem.

But tell me, Babuji, do you want it badly enough to pay me three rupees for stealing it without being seen?"

Ram Bharosa gave the boy a long, sad look. "You're a sharp boy," he said. "You'll come to a bad end. I'll give you two rupees."

"Three," said the boy.

"Two," said the old man.

"You don't really want it, I can see that," said the boy.

"Wretch!" said the old man. "Evil one! Darkener of my doorstep! Get me the umbrella and I'll give you three rupees."

Binya was in the forest glade where she had first seen the umbrella. No one came there for picnics during the monsoon. The grass was always wet and the pine needles were slippery underfoot. The tall trees shut out the light, and poisonous looking mushrooms, orange and purple, sprang up everywhere. However, it was a good place for porcupines, who seemed to like the mushrooms; and Binya was searching for porcupine quills.

The hill people didn't think much of porcupine quills, but far away in southern India the quills were valued as charms and sold at a rupee each. So Ram Bharosa paid a tenth of a rupee for each quill brought to him, and he in turn sold the quills at a profit to a trader from the plains.

Binya had already found five quills, and she knew there'd be more in the long grass. For once, she'd put her umbrella down. She had to put it aside if she was to search the ground thoroughly.

33

It was Rajaram's chance.

He'd been following Binya for some time, concealing himself behind trees and rocks—creeping closer whenever she became absorbed in her search. He was anxious that she should not see him and be able to recognize him later. He waited until Binya had wandered some distance from the umbrella. Then, running forward at a crouch, he seized the open umbrella and dashed off with it.

But Rajaram had very big feet. Binya heard his heavy footsteps and turned just in time to see him as he disappeared between the trees. She cried out, dropped the porcupine quills, and gave chase.

Binya was swift and sure-footed, but Rajaram had a long stride. All the same, he made the mistake of running downhill. A long legged person is much faster going up hill than down. Binya reached the edge of the forest glade in time to see the thief scrambling down the path to the stream. He had closed the umbrella so that it would not hinder his flight.

Binya was beginning to gain on the boy. He kept to the path, while she simply slid and leapt down the steep hillside. Near the bottom of the hill the path began to straighten out, and it was here that the long legged boy began to forge ahead again.

Bijju was coming home from another direction. He had a bundle of sticks which he'd collected for the kitchen fire. As he reached the path, he saw Binya rushing down the hill as though all the mountain spirits in Garhwal were after her.

"What's wrong?" he called. "Why are you running?"

Binya paused only to point at the fleeing Rajaram.

34

"My umbrella!" she cried. "He has stolen it!"

Bijju dropped his bundle of sticks and ran after his sister. When he reached her side he said, "I'll soon catch him!" and went sprinting away over the lush green grass. He was fresh and was soon well ahead of Binya, and gaining on the thief.

Rajaram was crossing the shallow stream when Bijju caught up with him. Rajaram was the taller boy, but Bijju was much stronger. He flung himself at the thief, caught him by the legs, and brought him down in the water. Rajaram got to his feet and tried to get away, but Bijju still had him by a leg. Rajaram overbalanced and came down with a great splash. He had let the umbrella fall. It began to float away on the current. Just then Binya arrived, flushed and breathless, but went dashing into the stream after the umbrella.

Meanwhile, the two boys swayed together on a rock, tumbled on to the sand, rolled over and over the pebbled bank until they were again threshing about in the shallows of the stream. The magpies, bulbuls, and other birds were disturbed, and flew away with cries of alarm.

Covered with mud, Rajaram lay flat on his back, exhausted, while Bijju sat astride him, pinning him down with his arms and legs. "Let me get up!" gasped Rajaram. "Let me go—I don't want your useless umbrella!"

"Then why did you take it?" demanded Bijju. "Come on, tell me why!"

"It was that skinflint Ram Bharosa," said Rajaram. "He told me to get it for him. He said if I didn't fetch it, I'd lose my job."

35

By early October the rains were coming to an end. The ferns turned yellow, and the sunlight on the green hills was mellow and golden like the limes on the small tree in front of Binya's home. Bijju's days were happy ones, as he came home from school, munching on roasted corn. Binya's umbrella had turned a pale milky blue and was patched in several places, but it was still the prettiest umbrella in the village, and she still carried it with her wherever she went.

The cold, cruel winter wasn't far off—but somehow October seems longer than other months, because it is a kind month: the grass is good to lie upon, the breeze is warm and gentle and pine scented. That October everyone seemed contented—everyone, that is, except Ram Bharosa.

The old man had by now given up all hope of ever possessing Binya's umbrella. He wished he had never set eyes on it. Because of the umbrella he had suffered the tortures of greed, the despair of loneliness. Because of the umbrella, people had stopped coming to his shop.

Ever since it had become known that Ram Bharosa had tried to have the umbrella stolen, the village people had turned against him and stopped trusting the old man. Instead of buying their soap and tea and matches from his shop, they preferred to walk an extra mile to the shops near the Tehri bus stand. Who would have dealings with a man who had sold his soul for an umbrella? The children taunted him, twisted his name around. From "Ram the Trustworthy" he became "Trusty Umbrella Thief".

The old man sat alone in his empty shop, listening to the eternal hissing of his kettle, and wondering if anyone would ever again step in for a glass of tea. Ram Bharosa had lost his own appetite, and ate and drank very little. There was no money coming in. He had his savings in a bank in Tehri, but it was a terrible thing to have to dip into! To save money, he had dismissed the blundering Rajaram. So he was left without any company. The roof leaked, the wind got in through the corrugated tin sheets —but Ram Bharosa didn't care.

Bijju and Binya passed his shop almost every day. Bijju went by with a loud but tuneless whistle. He was one of the world's whistlers; cares rested lightly on his shoulders. But, strangely enough, Binya crept quietly past the shop, looking the other way, almost as though she was in some way responsible for the misery of Ram Bharosa.

She kept reasoning with herself, telling herself that the umbrella was her very own, and that she couldn't help it if others were jealous of it. But had she loved the umbrella too much? Had it mattered more to her than people mattered? She couldn't help feeling that in a small way she was the cause of the sad look on Ram Bharosa's face and the ruinous condition of his shop. ("His face is a yard long," Bijju would say.) It was all due to his own greed, no doubt. But she didn't want him to feel too bad about what he'd done, because it made her feel bad about herself; and so she closed the umbrella whenever she came near the shop, opening it again only when she was out of sight.

One day towards the end of October, when she had ten paise in her pocket, she entered the shop and asked the old man for a toffee. She was Ram Bharosa's first customer in almost two weeks. He looked suspiciously at the girl. Had she come to taunt him, to flaunt the umbrella in his face? She had placed her coin on the counter. Perhaps it was a bad coin. Ram

Bharosa picked it up and bit it; he held it up to the light; he rang it on the ground. It was a good coin. He gave Binya the toffee.

Binya had left the shop when Ram Bharosa saw the closed umbrella lying on his counter. The blue umbrella he had always wanted was within his grasp at last! He had only to hide it at the back of this shop and no one would know that he had it—no one could prove that Binya had left it behind.

38

He stretched out his trembling, bony hand, and took the umbrella by the handle. He pressed it open. He stood beneath it, in the dark shadows of his shop, where no sun or rain could ever touch it.

"But I'm never in the sun or in the rain," he said aloud. "Of what use is an umbrella to me?"

And he hurried outside and ran after Binya.

"Binya, Binya!" he shouted. "Binya, you've left your umbrella behind!"

He wasn't used to running, but he caught up with her and held out the umbrella saying, "You forgot it—the umbrella!"

In that moment it belonged to both of them.

But Binya didn't take the umbrella. She shook her head and said, "You keep it. I don't need it any more."

"But it's such a pretty umbrella!" protested Ram Bharosa. "It's the best umbrella in the village."

"I know," said Binya. "But an umbrella isn't everything," And she left the old man holding the umbrella, and went tripping down the road, and there was nothing between her and the bright blue sky.

✳

Well, now that Ram Bharosa has the blue umbrella, (a gift from Binya, as he tells everyone) he is sometimes persuaded to go out into the sun or the rain and, as a result, he looks much healthier. Sometimes he uses the umbrella to chase away pigs or goats. It is always left open outside the shop, and anyone who wants to borrow it may do so; and so in a way it has become everyone's umbrella. It is faded and patchy, but it is still the best umbrella in the village.

People are visiting Ram Bharosa's shop again. Whenever Bijju or Binya stop for a cup of tea he gives them a little extra milk or sugar. They like their tea sweet and milky.

A few nights ago, a bear visited Ram Bharosa's shop. There had been snow on the higher ranges of the Himalayas, and the bear had been finding it difficult to obtain food; so it had come down to see what it could pick up near the village. That night it scrambled on to the tin roof of Ram Bharosa's shop and made off with a huge pumpkin which had been ripening on the roof. But in climbing off the roof the bear had lost a claw. The next morning Ram Bharosa found the claw outside the door of his shop. He picked it up and put it in his pocket. A bear's claw was a lucky find.

A day later, when he went into the market town, he took the claw with him, and left it with a silversmith, giving the craftsman certain instructions.

The silversmith made a locket for the claw; then he gave it a thin silver chain. When Ram Bharosa came again, he paid the silversmith ten rupees for his work.

The days were growing shorter and Binya had to be home a little earlier every evening. There was a hungry leopard at large and she couldn't leave the cows out after dark. She was hurrying past Ram Bharosa's shop when the old man called out to her.

"Binya, spare a minute! I want to show you something."

Binya stepped into the shop.

"What do you think of it?" asked Ram Bharosa, proudly showing her the silver pendant with the claw.

40

"It's so beautiful," said Binya, touching the claw and the silver chain.

"It's a bear's claw," said Ram Bharosa. "It's even luckier than a leopard's claw. Would you like to have it?"

"I have no money," said Binya.

"That doesn't matter. You gave me the umbrella—and I give you the claw! Come, let's see what it looks like on you." He placed the pendant on Binya—and indeed it looked very beautiful on her.

Ram Bharosa says he will never forget the smile she gave him when she left the shop! She was halfway home when she realized she had left the cows behind.

"Neelu, Neelu!" she called. "Oh, Gori!"

Then there was a faint tinkle of bells as the cows came slowly down the mountain path. In the distance she could her hear her mother and Bijju calling for her. She began to sing. When they heard her singing they knew she was safe and near.

Binya walked home through the darkening glade, singing of the stars. The trees stood still and listened to her, and the mountains were glad.

VALERIE SCHURER CHRISTLE

SIX INCHES TO ENGLAND

Thanks to Miss True's children

A **visitor** was due at school as soon as recess was over. Miss True told the children to act their best. It was an author and she was going to read them a story from England.

The author began, "The sisters Grimwade lived in the Wood. The Wood is nothing like the woods (with an 's') that grow in New Hampshire or Vermont . . . " Tyler raised his hand. Miss True shot him "a glance" and then smiled pleasantly as the author looked up.

"How far is it from New Hampshire to the Wood?" he asked.

The Wood, about which the author was reading, was in England. Did anyone know, she asked, how far it was from New Hampshire to England? Nathan, wanting to do his best, leaped from his desk and raced toward the large map that hung over the far end of the blackboard and covered all but the **X**, **Y**, and **Z** of the alphabet. Ruler in hand, he climbed on a chair and began his measurements. "It's exactly six inches!"

All the children were pleased to know the answer.

"*Thank you, Nathan.*" It would make a good story, the author thought. You could read it when you grew up, and had forgotten those days when distance had no meaning—nor "foreigners," nor "strangers".

A true story

42

THE TSAR AND THE SHIRT

Translated from a Russian tale
by Leo Tolstoy

Once upon a time there lived a Tsar who fell ill. He said, "Half of my kingdom will I give to anyone who cures me!" Then were assembled all the wise men of the kingdom who set about thinking how to cure the Tsar. (None of them knew for sure.) But one of the wise men said, "To cure the Tsar we must find a happy man, take his shirt from him, and put it on the Tsar. In this way the Tsar recovers!"

With that the Tsar commanded that a happy man be found. The Tsar's subjects searched the whole of the kingdom, far and wide, but such a man who was completely and altogether happy could not be found: one was rich, but in poor health. Another was healthy, but poor. Yet another was both healthy and wealthy, but had a rotten wife. Everyone had something to grumble about!

Tolstoy came from the Establishment of Russia. Yet he loved the peasant people and would spend days on end walking the road between Moscow and Kiev, listening to their witty tales. Tolstoy took special care to preserve their plain, direct manner of speaking.

*The greatest happiness
is to be satisfied with a little.*

RUSSIAN PROVERB

43

One day, however, while the *Tsarevich* was walking far from home he came upon a little *izbychka* and suddenly he heard someone say, "Thanks to God for this wonderful day! I did a little work, I had something to eat, and now I am going to have a nice and peaceful sleep. There is nothing more I want or need."

The *tsarevich* rejoiced! He immediately told the Tsar's messengers to go take off the man's shirt, to give him some money (whatever he wanted) and to take his shirt to the Tsar. Ax, how the messengers wanted the shirt for their Little Father. But when they came to the happy man, they found he had no shirt to wear!

Tsarevich: the Tsar's son

izbychka: the smallest of cottages where Russian peasants lived

In olden days peasants would affectionately refer to the Tsar as "Little Father."

The kypech appeared and bowed politely,
while the Tsar said nothing.

THE KYPECH AND THE TSAR

Based on an old Georgian tale

**here was**, there was, and yet there was not, a Tsar who once thought that God had given wisdom to him, alone. One day, however, word spread through the tsardom of the wisdom of a poor, one-eyed kypech. Feeling both curious and cross, the Tsar demanded the kypech be brought before him.

The kypech soon appeared and bowed politely—but the Tsar said nothing. The kypech bowed again even more reverently. Yet the Tsar only stared at him uncomfortably.

At long last, the Tsar raised one finger.

The kypech held up two.

The Tsar held up three.

Quickly the kypech made a fist.

With that, the Tsar reached out and grabbed an orange from the

Georgian tales always begin with the words, "There was, there was, and yet there was not."

kypech: a pedlar

Georgia is in the mountainous Caucasus region below Russia between the Black and Caspian Seas.

tattered basket slung around the neck of the poor, one-eyed kypech. The kypech, fumbling with the basket, reached into his pocket and pulled out an old crust of bread. Then to the amazement of all his courtiers the Tsar suddenly declared, "The kypech has won! He has more wisdom than me. Give him the half of my kingdom!"

The kypech bowed and went home.

The courtiers said to the Tsar (naturally not daring to say otherwise), "*Little Father*, you alone possess all the wisdom to the thrice ninth lands and to the thrice tenth tsardom. How is it the kypech won?"

To which the Tsar answered:

"I showed him one finger declaring that there is one God. He answered with two declaring that there is the Father, and the Son. When I replied with three fingers, the Father, the Son, and the Holy Ghost, he immediately closed his fist saying that these three are as one in the Trinity.

"Seeing his wisdom indeed surpassed mine in spiritual things, I then changed the subject to my power as Tsar. I took an orange from his basket declaring my ownership of all things in the kingdom. Yet, he gave me his last crust of bread, proving that I could not take away his humanity."

The courtiers naturally said nothing, but marvelled at the wisdom of the kypech—as great as any Tsar's.

By that time the kypech had arrived home eager to tell his wife the news. "My dear," said the poor one-eyed kypech to his wife, "I'm afraid

46

In olden times, the Tsar was often affectionately referred to as "Little Father."

In Tsarist times, the Tsar was the head of the Church, as well as the kingdom, thus he was supposedly not only the wisest, but holiest, man of all.

our Little Father has gone mad, for he just gave us half of his tsardom in exchange for an old crust of bread!"

The kypech went on to explain, "I went to the palace and bowed before the Tsar, but almost immediately I lost my temper!"

The wife of the poor, one-eyed kypech gasped!

"From the moment I appeared, our Little Father did nothing but stare at me. Thinking I was deaf, as well as half-blind, he said nothing, but held up one finger making fun of my infirmity. I didn't dare speak since he had not spoken first, so I held up two fingers assuring him that I may only see from one eye but, nonetheless, I do indeed have two!

"Yet he persisted mockingly and held up three, 'No, we have only three eyes between us!'

"Naturally, his arrogance made me angry, and before I knew what I was doing I held up my fist and shook it at him! He was so afraid he grabbed an orange to throw at me. But then, feeling sorry for him, I gave him my crust of bread and made peace. He was so relieved, he gave me half of his kingdom!"

The wife said nothing, only marvelling at the Tsar's stupidity—as great as any kypech's.

The king stepped forward.

THE KING AND THE LAMP

by Duncan Williamson

any, many years ago there was an old tinkerman. He wandered round the country making tin because in these days everything needed was made from tin. And everything he used to make his tin he carried on his back.

Some of the tools of his trade were shears for cutting the tin and a soldering bolt for soldering it. He went from place to place mending pots and kettles, ladles, toasters, and all these kinds of things. But—unlike any other old traveller—he was only by himself. He met other travellers along the way and they wondered why, but this old man had never got married.

So, one summer he would be in one place, the next summer he would be in another place and the next summer he would be in another—in villages and towns. But there was one particular town he liked better than

traveller: a Scottish gypsy. They were renowned not only for their storytelling, but for their skill as tinsmiths.

any other and he always used to come back, every year, because he got a lot of work there. And the funny thing was, something always drew him back—whether it was the town or whether it was because it was close to the king's palace, nobody will ever know.

But one day he landed back. Not far from the town was the palace. It sat up on a great big hill, and in the palace lived the king and the queen. The old man carried his tent on his back as well as his working things— his tools for making tin. He was quite happy when he landed back near the village and he put up his small tent. The next morning he walked into the village. It wasn't very big but he loved this village.

That night he sat up and he worked late. He made kettles, pots, ladles, spoons—everything he thought he could make. And the next morning he packed them all on his back and walked into the village. He met a lot of people along the way—people that he had known before and had done some jobs for. He asked them, "Have you got anything to mend?"

And they said, "Yes, we've got things to mend but we can't afford it."

"Do you want to buy something then—can I sell you a pot? Can I sell you a ladle? Can I sell you a toaster?" the tinkerman asked.

But he met the same problem all the way, wherever he went. And the old man began to think, 'Times must be really hard. Nobody seems to want my tinware anymore.' So at last he landed at the end of the village. An old woman lived there, and he had known her for years.

He said to her, "Are your kettles and pots needing mending, my old friend?"

She said, "Yes, old tinkerman, my kettles and pots need mending."

"Well," he said, "let me do them for you!"

"Well, you can do them for me but I'm sorry I can't pay you."

"Oh! Why can you no pay me? I'm sure I don't charge you very much *"no," here means "not"* for your kettles and pots. Pennies is all, I think."

"I couldn't pay you a penny, old man, I couldn't even pay you a penny."

"Well," he said, "how about a new pan?"

She said, "My pans are burned through." (Because tin pans in these days didn't last very long; they were only made of thin tin.) "We'd love to . . . but everyone here in the whole . . . old man, you'll no sell much here this time."

He said, "It's been a year since I've been here!"

"But," she said, "last year was different from this year."

"But why? Why was last year so different?"

"Well, our taxes have been raised since last year. Our king doesn't give us much chance. And the same thing happens in all the country and all the villages around. The king has made new laws and raised all our taxes. The farmers can't pay them; neither can the villagers pay their taxes to the landlords. And we're so poor that if things don't change, soon everybody'll have to be like you, old traveller man—we'll have to pack up and go on the road because we can't afford it."

"Well," said the old tinker, "bad business for you is bad business for me. Why doesn't somebody do something about it?"

"What can we do? We can't go to the king and tell him to stop raising our taxes. He takes three-quarters of the corn from the farmers, three-quarters of everything they grow, if they don't have any money to pay his taxes. Then the landlord who we work for does the same with us, and we're so poor we're hardly able to survive."

"Well," said the old traveller man, "there must be something done about this."

She said, "There's nobody who can do anything about it. Because we don't want to lose our homes. We don't want to lose our village. We don't want to lose our land—there's nothing we can do."

So the old traveller man had tried his best but he never made one single penny that day. He walked home very sad to his own little tent which he had camped outside the village. And he kept in his mind the thought that something had to be done. "Nobody was going to do it, so," he said, "it's up to me. I'll have to do it. Because it's in my interest to do it in the first place."

Then he lay all night in his bed, his little bed of straw on the ground in his tent. And he thought and he thought and he thought of a plan to try to help the villagers and the small farmers around the district who were so good to him. . . . And then he came up with the answer: the king must be made to understand—and he—a poor tinker, a traveller tinsmith, was the very person, the one who was going to make the king understand the predicament in the village!

The very next morning he got up bright and early and had a little breakfast which was very meagre at this time because he had made no money in the village. He packed his camp on his back, and his tools, and made his way through the village to the king's palace. But he didn't go straight to the palace. On the way from the village there was a road that led up

52

through a forest, and then there was a large driveway that led up to a hill, and on the hill was the king's palace.

The story I'm telling you goes back nearly seven to eight hundred years ago. In these days there were lots of trees, hundreds of trees! The whole country was overrun with them. There was more wood than anything else, and the old tinker had little trouble finding a place to put up his tent and sticks for his fire. So where did he choose to put his tent? On the drive going to the king's palace! It was nothing like the drives you have today —it was just a track right through the wood, beautiful and better made than any in the village. In the village they had no roads. But going to the king's palace they had a road made especially for the king's horses and carriages to pass along. The old tinkerman chose a piece of land as close to the palace and as close to the road as he could find!

53

Then he put up his tent and kindled his fire and started to work on his tinware. But he hadn't been working very long, when who came along but the king's caretaker. And he saw the old traveller man on the pathway.

"Get out of here!" he said. "Old m— Who are you! And what are you doing here?"

"I'm doing nothing. I am at my work and at my job."

"But, you can't, man. You can't work and kindle a fire here, this is the king's—the driveway to the king's palace!"

"Well I don't care, the driveway to the king's palace or not. I've pitched my tent here and I'm making my tin here. I've got to make my livelihood."

So the caretaker who was guarding the palace tried his best to get rid of the old man. But no way, the old man wouldn't move.

"Well," he said, "I'll soon find somebody that'll shift you."

Up the driveway he goes and he sees some of the king's guards. (Now, there were no police in the land in these days, and any soldiers that were available belonged to the king, and the king could command these soldiers to do anything that he wanted.) And the first person the caretaker of the king's land met was the captain of the king's soldiers.

54

He said to the caretaker, who was out of breath by this time for he had to run nearly a mile and a half, "Stop, man, what's the trouble?"

He said, "The trouble" (panting) "the trouble is—there's an old tinkerman on the driveway leading to the palace. And he's got his fire kindled! He's got his tent there and he's busy making tinware. And the king is due to go to the village in a very short time!"

"But," said the king's guard, "that's no problem. We'll soon square it up."

He called to five of his troop. They jumped on their horses and rode down the drive. They arrived and the old tinkerman was busy—he had his fire going—working on his tinware.

The king's officer jumped off his horse along with his soldiers and commanded the old man to get moving away from the place because the king was due to pass down this way in a very little time.

But the old man said, "No. I too am a subject of the king. He's my king as well as yours. I don't own any land—I don't have any land—but any land that belongs to the king belongs to me. Because he's my king! And if he's my king and I'm one of his subjects, I'm entitled to park my tent on his land and make my living as well as the next person."

As he was an old man, the guards did not want to be rough or manhandle him, so they tried to argue with him. They argued and tried to get rid of him when who should appear, right at that very moment, but the king in his carriage! Ahead of the coach rode two or three couriers. When the king came to the six horses and his officers standing in the road he ordered the driver to pull up.

He opened the door of his coach and said, "What is the hold-up here?" And then he saw the fire, he saw the smoke, and he saw the tent of the old man. "What's going on here?" said the king.

They lowered the steps from the coach and the king stepped down and walked out onto the driveway. The captain of the king's officers bowed to the king and said, "Your Majesty, we don't want you to see this."

"Why not? Why shouldn't I see? Wha-wha-what's going on? What's the trouble here? Why is my driveway . . . I am late as it is, to make an appearance in the village."

"Well, Sir," he said, "It's one of your subjects."

"One of my subjects?" said the king. "What is the trouble then?"

He said, "Sir, it's an old tinkerman."

"An old tinkerman? Well," he said, "I'm sure you are a troop of soldiers —I don't think you need to be afraid of an old tinkerman."

"But, Sir," he said, "he's got his fire kindled and he's got his tent up and he's making—he's making his livelihood on your driveway!"

"Oh well," said the king (chuckling), "that I would love to see! Move —step back!" And the king walked forward.

Sure enough there was the old tinkerman making things he would need to sell. But the thing he was specially making was a lamp—the most beautiful lamp. And he was just about finished with it when the king stepped forward. And the king was amazed: he saw the common fire, he saw the common tent, and he saw a piece of leather laid out, and all the working tools that the old traveller man had used. The king had never in his life ever seen anything like this! The king had seen lamps and seen kettles, but he never had an idea where they came from.

So the king was mesmerized and so happy to see this that he told everyone, "Stay back for a moment, please, just stay back for a moment!"

Everyone had to obey the king. The captain of the guards couldn't do anything. They stood back and held the horses. And the king sat down on his hunkers beside the old man. He watched the old man. The old man paid no attention to the king, never letting on that he knew this was anybody other than a spectator, till he finished the lamp. Then he polished it, and the old man looked up. . . . He said, "Your Majesty, I am making a lamp. A special lamp."

The king looked, "Is it finished?"

And the old man said, "Yes, my lord, it's finished."

"Well, you know," he said, "my lamps in my palace are not very good and I think that's a better lamp than any I've ever seen. How much would you take for that lamp from me?"

"Oh! Your Majesty, I would never take anything from you. I just want you not to be angry with me for staying on your ground!"

"No," said the king, "I'm not angry with you. And I'm willing to pay for your lamp. I get paid for everything I do. Why should you not be paid?"

And the king put his hand into his own pocket and took out four gold crowns and put them in the old man's hand. "Now," he said, "I'm giving you these four gold crowns for your lamp because I want it for myself, for my own room, and I hope it works! But to be fair to you, if it doesn't work the way I want it to, you're going to be in trouble. So that I can find you again, you stay where you are and don't move! You've got my permission to stay here."

The king took his lamp in his hand and he walked to his coach and bade all his soldiers and everybody to go about their business.

The king told his footman, "Drive on!" He put his lamp in his coach with him. "That," he said, "I'm taking back," and he waved to the old man through the coach window. The old tinkerman was quite happy. "Now," he said, "my task is half done!"

So the tinkerman stayed there all that day. The king went about his business: visited the village and did all that he wanted to do, met all the people he wanted to see in the village, and the moment that he returned to his palace in his coach, the first thing he took out with him was his lamp. Into the palace he went and met his queen who was happy to see him returned. She said, "You're home, my lord!"

"Yes, my darling, I'm home."

"But what is that you have in your hand?"

"Oh, this is something special, my dear. This is a lamp!"

"Oh, I would love to see it working."

The king said, "Well, it will be in our bedroom tonight. We will have the most beautiful light that anybody ever had!"

Now the lamps in these days weren't very popular because you couldn't afford lamps—not the way the old tinker could make them. You had to be very rich to be able to buy a good lamp.

So late that afternoon the king called for the headman in the castle and told him to fill his lamp and have it ready—that he and his queen would have their lamp while they had their evening meal. Now the old tinker-man was in his tent and he kindled his fire, made a little meal to himself, and then sat back and waited. And he waited. He knew what he was wait-ing for.

Back in the palace it was evening and all this *beautiful food* was brought forward to the king and the queen, and placed before them for their sup-per. Evening in olden times came very quickly because these old palaces were all built of solid rock and stone, and windows were just barred. So the king and queen were dining and they had a few lights going.

The king said, "Bring more light! Bring me my lamp, my special lamp that I got this moring as a present from my old friend, the tinkerman! Bring my lamp and put it beside my meal where I can see what I'm eating!"

In these days they filled the lamps with tallow, common oil made from melted down animal fat. And they placed what you call "rushie wicks" in the lamps made from rushes, the insides of rushes plaited together. They didn't have cotton because cotton wasn't invented at that time, so they took the natural wild rushes and split them, and took the centers from the rushes and wove them together to make wicks. To make a large flame you would use maybe five—to make a small flame for a night light, maybe one. Or if you wanted brighter light you used two. So they had special people to make these rushie wicks; not anybody could make one. It could have been a turn for a butler or maybe the cook who made rushie wicks for the lamp. . . .

The lamp was placed before the king, right beside his supper. The king was delighted because it was blazing and he could see all around him! Shadows had been climbing up the walls; then they disappeared as everything was lit up inside the palace chamber. The king said to himself, "That is a beautiful lamp. I surely underpaid the old man who made that lamp for me."

But as he was eating his supper, the funniest thing happened, the tallow in the lamp began to leak out and spread across the table. The king was halfway through his meal when he looked and saw the tallow leaking from the lamp, floating right out over the table. And the light of the flame began to get lower and lower as the tallow escaped. The king looked —and the lamp went out!

The king was angry—more than angry—because he had told everyone about his special lamp and then it went out! He was so angry he couldn't eat his supper. And he got so wild he began to shout and walk round the inside of the palace chamber.

"Go!" he said to the captain of the guard, "and bring me that old tinkerman at once! Bring him before me! I'll have his head for this!"

So naturally, the old tinkerman was waiting. He saw the guards coming and he knew what was up. They arrested him immediately and fetched him before the king. And he hung his head before the king, right in the king's chamber.

By this time the king's anger had subsided a wee bit. The king was up;

he'd only half finished his supper. The queen had retired to her chamber.

"You call yourself a tinsmith?" he said to the old tinker.

"Yes, my lord. I call myself a tinsmith."

"And you made the lamp?"

"Yes, my lord, I made the lamp."

"And you told me that it was the best lamp that you ever made?"

"Yes, my lord, it was the best lamp I ever made. I never made a lamp before like it."

"And you promised me that it would give me light—better light than any other lamp that you'd ever made?"

"Yes, my lord, I said it would give you better light than any lamp I'd ever made."

"Well," said the king, "look at my table! And I never finished my meal because of your lamp leaking! It destroyed the table . . . and upset me— I never even finished my meal! And you call yourself a tinsmith!"

"Well, Your Majesty, my dear lord, my king," he said, "have I your permission to speak in my own way?"

"Yes, you can speak in your own way and tell me why that lamp is not fit for me!"

"Well, Your Majesty, I work hard, and I made sure that the lamp was fit for you, but it's not my fault."

"It's not your fault! Why is it not your fault? You made it!"

"Your Majesty, my king, my lord, I made it. But I couldn't make it any better than I made it. If there's anyone to blame, it's not me. It's the man who gives me the tin to make my lamp that's at fault, not me. If he'd given me good tin to make a good lamp for you, my lord, I would have made a good lamp."

"Well," the king said, "there could be something in that. Go find the village tinsmith," he told the captain of the guards, "and bring him before me this moment!"

Naturally, the captain of the guards wasn't long going to the village and he brought back this tinsmith. And he stood before the king and bowed.

61

The king said, "You are the tinsmith of the village?"

He said, "Yes I am. I am the tinsmith of the village."

"Did you sell this old tinsmith some tin today?"

"Yes, my lord, I sold him some tin."

"Well," he said, "he made me a lamp and the lamp is hopeless because your tin is hopeless."

"Well, my lord, if my tin is hopeless it's not my fault."

"Why is it not your fault? You are the man who sells the tin to people who make these things that everyone needs, and you turn around and tell me that it's not your fault?"

"No, my lord, it's not my fault."

"Well, whose fault is it?"

He said, "It's the man from the foundry who produces my tin that's at fault, not me."

So the king sent two guards to the smelter in the small iron foundry who made tin. The man was arrested and brought to the palace. . . .

His Majesty said, "Did you sell some tin to the tin dealer who sold this tin to the tinkerman who made my lamp?"

"Yes, my lord, I did. I supply all his tin."

He said, "Why is your tin not fit to make a lamp for me?"

"Well, my lord, if the tin's no fit enough, it's not me to blame."

"Well," he said, "who is to blame? Someone has to stand accused for the mistake that was made for me!"

"Well, my lord, it's not my fault."

"Whose fault is it?" said the king.

"The fault must lie with the man who makes my bellows to blow my fire to make my heat to make my tin!"

"Well," said the king, "fetch him! Bring him here."

Naturally, off went the king's guards again and brought back the bellows-maker who made the bellows for pumping the air into the fire foundry to melt the ore to make the tin. And he was brought before the king.

The king said, "Step before me! Bellows-maker, you're charged with…" and he told him the whole story, as I'm telling you.

The bellows-maker said, "My lord and my king, you must forgive me! Because. . ."

"Why should I forgive you! You're the cause of all my trouble and the trouble of these other men who stand before me. They're condemned! They're going to suffer."

The bellows-maker said, "Well, my lord, my king, it's not my fault."

"Well," he said, "whose fault is it?"

"My lord, it's the man in the tannery's fault who sells me my skins to make my bellows." (Now all these bellows that pumped the fire with air were made from skins.)

The king said, "Get the man here from the tannery at this moment! I want to get to the end of this. Bring him here before me!"

Naturally, the man from the tannery was sent for who had tanned all the skins and made the leather that was used in the bellows to blow the fire to melt the ore to make the tin for the old tinkerman. And they were all before the king. So the man from the tannery was brought forward before the king.

The king accused him straightaway and said, "Look. . ." and he told him the story I'm telling you. "You are a man of the tannery?"

"Yes, my lord, I am from the tannery."

"You make the skins and tan the skins that make this man's bellows, that this man uses to melt this ore to make tin to sell to the tinsmith, who sold it to the tinker who made my lamp—and my lamp leaks on my table and upsets my supper?"

"Yes," says the tanner, "it's true. But, my lord, it's not my fault."

"Then, who's at fault! Someone stands condemned for this thing!"

And the man from the tannery said, "My lord, it's not me. My lord, it's the farmer who sends me the animals who I get the skins from."

"Well, bring the farmer to me! Immediately! I must get to the end of this, to the bottom of this thing tonight!"

So naturally, the farmer was sent for and he stood before the king and the king told him the story I'm telling you.

"You are the farmer who supplies skins to the tannery?"

"Yes, my lord, my king, I am."

"The tanner supplies them to the bellows-maker, and he sells bellows

to the man who melts the ore, and the man who melts the ore makes tin to supply tin to the tinsmith, and the tinsmith supplies it to this old tinker who made my lamp that destroyed my evening meal?"

"Yes, my lord, that's true."

"Well, why is it that your skins are not good enough?"

"My lord, and my king, I hope you will forgive me."

"Forgive you for what? I know I shan't forgive you!" said the king.

"My lord, there is no one at fault if I must tell the truth before my king," and he bowed. "Your Majesty, if the skins don't work to make the bellows, and the bellows don't work to heat the iron, and if the iron doesn't work to make the tin, and the tin doesn't work well enough to supply the tinsmith who sells it to the old tinkerman to make your lamp, then you're at fault!"

"Me," said the king, "I am at fault?"

"Yes, my king and my lord. You probably will have my head for this, but I have to tell you—you are at fault."

"And why," said the king, "am I at fault? You mean to tell me I'm at fault for the lamp that I never saw before that spills oil on my table and destroys my evening meal! I'm at fault?"

"Yes, my king, you're at fault."

"Well, tell me truthfully why am I at fault?"

"Well, my lord, to begin with, I grow *little* grain and three-quarters of that goes to you. With what I've got left I'm not able to feed my animals through the winter. Their skins are so poor that they're not even fit to make a bellows to blow a fire to heat some ore and make some tin to sell to a tinsmith to make a lamp for yourself."

The king said, "Is that the truth?"

"Yes," he said, "that's the truth."

The king sat back and thought. And he thought for a while. He turned round and said, "Gentlemen, come, gather round and sit here beside me."

And he said to the old tinkerman, "You are the one who taught me to be a real king! From now on, no more taxes on the farmers! What they grow they can keep it to themselves, for what good is it being a king to rule over people who can't even make something for me that I need, because of my own fault!"

65

And from that day on to this day, the king laid no more taxes on the farmers, and they produced grain and they produced animals and produced skins for the bellows-maker. The farmers produced the greatest of skins and these were given to the bellows-maker. And the bellows-maker made bellows past the common, and these were used in the foundries to blow air into the furnaces to melt iron, and the iron was made into beautiful sheets of tin, and the beautiful sheets of tin were sold to the tinsmiths, and the tinsmiths made the most beautiful things. And for evermore everyone was happy—except the king. He was left with his lamp that leaked from the old tinkerman!

And that is the last of my story.

Duncan Williamson is a traveller, and is one of Scotland's most loved storytellers. Storytelling is a heritage that goes back literally centuries in his family.

This slightly abridged version of "The King and The Lamp" was used with his warm and wholehearted permission. We only regret that you are not able to hear his lyrical Scottish brogue telling it.

*Reagan was stretched out on the soft oriental
carpet in front of the Finnish fireplace.*

THE SUMMER PALACE

Adapted from a Russian boy's reminiscences

AUGUST, 1994

THE SUMMER PALACE, MISKHOR CRIMEA

Like a plump clump of curious old *babushkas*, five fat blackbirds sat chattering somewhere in the cool, dark woods. Farther off, in one of the small, hidden gardens, came the soft, slicing sound of a gardener trimming the hedges as rhythmically as if he were a pastor bestowing a blessing. But all these things—the gifts of another beautiful morning, the birds' chattering, the wind's sighing, and the sea's laughter—all went unnoticed by the young, pale boy who sat squinting uncomfortably into the bright morning light. He was watching two of the palace guards walking in the distance along a narrow, stone seawall. One of them was singing sentimentally as Russians, accustomed to too little sleep, and too many memories, often do.

babushka:grandmother.

Crimea is a beautiful and very old land which lies in the Black Sea. It is now a part of Ukraine.

68

Pahsmatree!: Look!

Krym: Crimea.

There is a famous painting by the Russian painter, Ilya Repin of the Zaporozhye Cossacks writing a mocking letter to the Turkish Sultan at a time when Russia was at odds with Turkey.

The song rolled off the backs of the soft blue waves and washed around the boy's slender feet, but quickly drew away, afraid of his melancholy face.

The boy's bodyguard sat a little way off, out of his view, but hearing, too, the careless voice of his comrade who was supposed to be on duty. He envied his abandon. Who could not help but sing when August was pouring out her beauty on everything? Only a fool wouldn't feel like singing here in the Garden of Schai`ir! The guard looked again at the melancholy boy and sighed. Out at sea the white-headed eagles were soaring in the morning breeze. The sun played with the flowers and leaves, and the tall, tender grasses along the beach. It sparkled on the waves and illumined the deep. At last, it ascended once again to heaven from the golden domes of the proud cathedral, resting high above them on the mountain peak.

"*Pahsmatree!*" yelled the boy's bodyguard suddenly. "A little sailing ship on the horizon, Maxime Yuriavich! Do you suppose it belongs to midgets —or do you think the Turkish Sultan is trying once again to capture *Krym*? Shall we write a nasty letter to him, Maxime Yuriavich?"

Maxime looked up, but said nothing. All that morning he had been thinking nothing but serious thoughts and they had exhausted him. He had no strength left to act properly. Instead, he got up sullenly and started back for the palace.

"Maxime Yuriavich! Why are you going inside on such a beautiful day? Why don't you stay outside and play?"

"With whom? *You?!*" Maxime complained as he disappeared past the large wooden gate into the Summer Palace. The guard followed obediently, but was very annoyed at the foolish boy. Why was he so difficult?

What boy could possibly be unhappy who had gone to bed one night a pauper and awakened the next day a prince? "Ax!" thought the guard to himself. "This is one boy I do not understand! His father is a president; they are living here in the Garden of Schai`ir and what? He acts like he's in prison. Such a boy! And now I must watch over him inside. I am the prisoner, if there ever was one, and I am only trying to do my job! Ah, such a boy. . . ." The guard hurried along closing the gate behind him.

The Summer Palace was just as you would imagine a Russian palace to be. It had soft pink walls that reminded you of the pictures of the frosting on the *tsarevich's* cake in the tale of *The Frog Princess*. It had large, ornamental windows that faced out to the sea. And, of course, it had enough rooms so that even if twenty-six very important, portly personages should show up at a moment's notice, they would each be *properly* accommodated.

tsarevich: the son of a tsar

There were rooms with fireplaces, rooms with thick carpets, and rooms with satin draperies that billowed gracefully in the morning breeze. And, last, but not least, there were rooms for *meeting people*—very important people—for they were the only ones who had ever come to the Summer Palace. They came (as you can imagine) to consider important considerations, to question important questions, and to conclude important conclusions. When they were done, they felt very important indeed. Each important piece of paper was stamped (loudly) with a bright, red stamp, and then carefully folded and sealed with a thick, red seal.

But to Maxime, these things only meant that *he* was now no longer as important as he used to be. Of course, that wasn't really so. It just seemed that way which, to Maxime, was as bad as if it were really true. In fact, he

was still like every Russian boy—idolized by his father. But now his father was a president and there was nothing he could do about it. He made his way past the huge wooden doors of the library where his father was meeting with his advisors. Would he see his father tonight at their evening meal, he wondered wistfully? "I will demand it!" he thought miserably. Even Maxime knew it was truly miserable being a demanding boy, but it frightened him even more to think of growing up and having to leave the attention behind. Would anyone (other than his father or mother) ever think he was important?

70

He often demanded that his bodyguard treat him like he was important, but it wasn't the same thing. Even when he called out to his bodyguard angrily, he didn't *feel* important. The guard's reply was always the same. "You may call me whatever you wish Maxime Yuriavich! You may even call me a pot. Just do not put me into the fire!"

This is a well-known Russian saying.

It wasn't as if Maxime didn't know that it felt much better to be good than to be difficult. He just somehow couldn't always remember how to do it. Just when he would decide that he wanted to be good, like a great gust of wind blowing away a paper, the thought would be gone and instead he'd be difficult. . . .

Someone had left the door ajar into the Great Room. Maxime looked in and smiled his only smile since they had arrived. Reagan, Maxime's great Italian mastiff, was stretched out on the soft oriental carpet in front of the great Finnish fireplace. The fireplace had been a gift to General Secretary Khrushchev from the President of Finland. It had caused no little excitement when it arrived, piece by piece, in heavy wooden boxes accompanied by Finnish craftsmen who wore white gloves to assemble the handsome blue and white tiles. Everyone could see they must be professionals. Ever after, all those responsible for cleaning the fireplace had worn white gloves and acted very professionally. Reagan, however, having chosen this spot for his morning nap, was wholly unaware that he was drooling contentedly in his sleep.

71

Sensing the presence of someone, Reagan growled, opened one eye, and lifted his huge black head off the carpet. His jowl, hanging heavily down from his mouth, made it look even bigger than it was. Seeing it was only Maxime, Reagan let out a peaceful grunt and fell back to sleep.

"Let him be!" thought Maxime triumphantly.

Maxime knew the guards were terrified of his big black dog and would not be able to remove him without making a scene. Whoever had left the door open was sure to be sacked. The possibility of the guilty guard's fate temporarily cheered him. "Why," he reasoned sullenly, "should I be the only miserable one at the Summer Palace?" But his boyish joy did not last long. The guard would be sent home among his friends, while he, Maxime, would still have no one to play with! "If only one night," he thought, "I could have dinner with my father, then he would see my misery and do something for me!"

That night, both of Maxime's wishes came true. The guilty guard was dismissed and Maxime was told his father would be eating with the family.

"Papa! I must speak with you immediately!" demanded Maxime before they had scarcely been seated. His mother lifted her beautiful black eyes, but said nothing while his sister was busy eyeing the food on the table.

"What about, Maxime?" answered his father quietly. His father was tired after a long day of meetings but, even so, it was his manner to speak calmly to his restless and serious son.

"I want to speak with you about all that is wrong!"

"I'm listening."

Maxime spoke very quickly. His voice was still thin and high. It would be several more summers before it assumed the deep tone of a confident Russian man. Nonetheless, there was a definite firmness in all that he said. His father listened patiently.

Maxime's father was the first man who had ever been elected president in the Republic of Crimea. Crimea had been conquered by Catherine the Great in the 1780s and, ever after, it had been ruled by *tsars* and *tsarinas* until the days of the communist regime. And so for the people of Crimea, the coming of democracy was like a dream that had finally come to be. It brought with it great hopes and possibilities. But for Maxime, it was altogether frightening and so, more often than not, his words were filled with complaints! Why was *his* father responsible for the well-being of an entire country? How could he change anything so big? What if he made a mistake?

Maxime paused briefly as one of the household staff brought in their salads—mushrooms and tomatoes prepared in vinegar, with huge chunks of dark rye bread laden with wedges of butter as thick as cheese. Once again Maxime began to speak—even more quickly—fearing his father might at any moment be called away. Had his father not promised to make life better for ordinary people? Were not he and his sister, and his mother and father still just ordinary people? How would people know that his father had not forgotten them, if they were living in a palace while everyone else was still poor?

While these were all the words Maxime *said*, if you could have heard, instead, what he was *thinking*, this is what it would have been. "How will *my friends* know that I have not forgotten them, if we are living in a palace while they are still poor?" And this, he suddenly realized, was what was making him so miserable! But, as so often happens when you're thinking deep and serious thoughts (as Maxime had been thinking that morning), he *also remembered* that there had been other thoughts that had made him think that there might be a way not to be miserable.

Maxime had run out of breath and was now silent, anxiously trying to remember a thought that had managed to escape before it had told him how to be happy. What was it? . . .

His father had carefully laid down his knife and fork, and looked attentively at Maxime and said, "And what would make you happy?"

"I want my friends," he burst out suddenly, "all of the friends who supported us, to come to the palace with me! Say 'yes,' Father . . . *please*! Just for the summer holiday. If you truly believe what you have promised the people then you must say 'yes,' Father!"

Suddenly Maxime realized that was it—the morning thought that had escaped! He felt happy. No, that was not it. He felt triumphant and was sure his father would praise him for such a great idea. He even hoped the guards had overheard what he said. What a relief, Maxime thought, to have found the solution for his misery.

"Maxime!" said his father sternly. "That is impossible! How could you ask me such a thing? You know that no one except high ranking officials are allowed inside the palace! How could you think so recklessly! Do you expect the KGB to look after screaming children? No, Maxime, you are not right to ask me this thing! I suppose you think the guards would join in your playing cowboys and Indians!"

Even as he disagreed, the lonely president-father felt horribly imprisoned in a world he was still just only learning how to live in. How was it that he, the president of an entire country, was powerless to grant his son's request? How could he make his son see that he was no longer a free man, but owned by his responsibilities?

How clearly he remembered these children running through the streets, shouting his name, putting up signs, and then standing proudly by as the name of their street was changed from Prospect to VICTORY BOULEVARD! And now these children and their struggling parents were waiting for him to change their lives! What an overwhelming thought! The lonely president was brought back from his far-off thoughts by the sound of his son's pleading, "How can I believe in your ideals if you will not allow me to participate in them? You are the President of Crimea! Which kind of Crimea will it be?!"

"That is enough, Maxime. We will discuss it further in the morning."

No more was said. Maxime went off to his room when his father was called away to the phone. His mother and sister finished their meal alone.

That night Maxime lay awake unable to sleep. He was still not used to a soft bed, or sheets. He was not used to living in the big, lonely palace when all his friends were living in crowded, one-room flats; or to having too much to eat when others went hungry. There was, as well, an even more frightening thought that troubled Maxime. It was the awful feeling of being envied, of your life making others feel small and unhappy. Even worse, it terrified him to think he might one day forget them! With such strange feelings, it was impossible for Maxime to think about sleeping.

He thought instead about what it would be like if his father said, 'yes.' He imagined arriving at each of his friend's houses in a black limousine. He would order his driver to drive slowly down the street. Maxime would sit very still and act seriously. The neighbors would be peeking out of their windows, he knew, and wondering who was coming! They would be scream-ing and shouting and wondering what it could all mean! Maxime would stay calm and act with dignity. When his friends finally recognized him, they would surely think how much he was becoming like a president!

First of all, Maxime would order the driver to go to Irina's. Her moth-er mended clothes for a living. They had very little and, as is the case with people who have very little, they never thought about having much as it would only stand the risk of being taken away. Maxime would order his bodyguard to go to Irina's door and fetch her, to bow politely and to call her by her proper name, . . . "Irina Ivanova, please come with me!"

Maxime imagined the same scene over and over again for each of his friends: Luba and Misha and Sasha; Alexi from Belorussia who walked with a limp; his two Ukrainian friends Vladimir and Nikolai, as well as

his new friend Volodya, whose father was Greek. Finally there would be Antosha, his special Tatar friend whose family had only recently returned to Crimea to reclaim the house that had once belonged to his grandfather.

Maxime was not aware of the fact that his hands were clenched into tight little fists. "I will show my father!" he vowed determinedly, *"I will make Father see."* Maxime buried his head in the mountain of pillows, not sure if what he felt was anger or fear. And then, as happened every night now before he fell asleep, he remembered his father calling him into his new office the morning of his inauguration. People had been rushing here and there but he had ordered them all to leave. Maxime had hardly recognized his father's face. It was strangely sad, as if someone had just played a mean trick on him.

"Maxime!" he had said, "Your decisions and the way you behave no longer affect only you. You must consider their effect on everyone, including me. When you act naughtily they will be glad, and when you act well, your brightest deeds will cause envy and fear, and perhaps even hate. Do you understand what I am saying?"

Maxime had never been sure who the "they" was his father was referring to. He only knew his life had completely changed. It was as if he was being taken away from his father and given to a stranger.

Maxime knew he could no longer cry, for he was now thirteen. Would his mother be coming to check on him? He left the small light on on his bedside table and, at some point, finally fell asleep.

✦

76

There is a Russian saying, "This life is a terrible trick!"

It was late when Maxime awakened the next morning. The previous day had exhausted him and now he lay on the bed struggling to be more awake than asleep. He moved restlessly under the bed coverings, but he was still half dreaming. He even thought he heard the limousines arriving, but why would they be out so early in the morning? His heart leaped, but then he realized where he was and remembered his dream of the night before.

At the same time the red phone in his father's conference room was ringing. There were no less than six phones in each of his father's offices which his secretary was responsible for tending, but when the red phone rang no one ever answered but the president himself. President Meshkov answered immediately even though he was in the midst of an important discussion with his advisors. He then ended the conversation quickly and excused himself from the meeting. His advisors frowned disapprovingly, but said nothing. On his way out, President Meshkov gave an order to the bodyguard but the advisors could not hear what he had said.

The President went only as far as the next room, to the large open window from which he could look out on the palace entrance. The two shiny black limousines had arrived and two KGB guards were dutifully tending the doors. Though she was dressed in a thin cotton skirt and worn sweater vest, the President thought Irina looked like a perfect little princess. Luba stood beside her holding her hand for security, as Misha, Sasha, Vladimir, Nikolai, Volodya and Antosha crowded behind.

In the coming years Maxime would have many lessons to learn, and many difficult days, but for now he had captured a very good thought and had turned it into a reality. That summer, for the only time in their lives,

Maxime's friends would have rooms and beds of their own. They would eat fruit and cheese from little china plates. There would be fresh fish and meat, as much as they pleased. They all would be called by their proper names and watched over while they played. The sea, not sirens, would sing them to sleep—and by day they would run through the halls of the palace playing cowboys and Indians, and laughing loudly.

They lived, for a few days at least, as a sometimes naughty, but otherwise good boy, living in a complicated world, believed life was really meant to be.

This is the true story of Maxime Meshkov and his father, former President Yury Aleksandrovich Meshkov. Only Maxime's friends' names have been changed. It is true that his friends came from all backgrounds and, like the Meshkovs, had always been poor. While the Meshkovs did go to the Summer Palace in the summer of 1994 for a rest, at Maxime's request the family lived the rest of the year in the same small flat they had always lived in, rather than moving into the presidential palace in Simferopol.

Eight children stayed at the Summer Palace the entire month of August. The fairy tale-like request was the first in the history of the Palace.

THE LOVED CHILD

A story from the Isle of Unst

On a wee island far away, a young man and his wife lived by the sea and worked in the fields to make a simple living. They had a bonny, wee babe whom they wrapped in a warm blanket and placed amid the singing grasses while they worked each day.

One day a sea eagle circled overhead longingly. Suddenly, the father looked up to see it flying away, and there was no mistake, in his talons was the blanket. The father's heart sank. He ran with all his strength toward the sea to where a boy sat working. "Up, lad!" yelled the man and together the two set off in the boy's boat toward the Isle of Fetlar. There, on a rocky peak, the bird had landed with the blanket still held in its beak.

The sea was favorable and the waves raced them on their way. When they reached the isle, the boy, whose strength was greater, climbed and ran, scrambling until, at last, he slowed his pace to keep from frightening the bird to some farther place. Yet the eagle neither flew away nor touched the babe. *He longed only to behold the child's sweet face.*

ᵍEach spring, the father would bring his daughter over the sea where they'd climb the steep grade, 'til they reached the top where the child would play. And the great bird would sit and watch as contentedly as one praying.

The Isle of Unst is the northernmost island of the small group of islands called the Shetland Islands, just north of the Orkney Islands which are just north of Scotland.

PETER FERBER

The boys sat talking things over.

LA LEÇON

Adapted from the French tale by Henri Pourrat

It so happened in the province of Auvergne, on the estate of a wealthy lord, that the same day the lord's wife bore him a little son, the wife of the lord's hunter gave birth to a son as well. The hunter lived in a small cottage on the estate and kept his lord well provided with game. As was common in those days, the lady of the castle gave her son to be nursed by the woman of the cottage. And so the lord's son and the hunter's son grew up before the same hearth. When they grew older, they roamed the fields and woods together, hunting for nests and rabbits' burrows, or scrambling beneath hedgerows and over streams, as truly as if they were brothers. Yet in truth, the one was always "the little lord", and the other "Jean-Pierre, the boy." There was no use arguing about it. What could not be changed, could not be changed, and Jean-Pierre felt no less alive for his lot.

This, however, greatly bothered the lord's son, for he could neither understand nor feel his foster brother's happiness. And while his parents daily reminded him that he was Jean-Pierre's "superior", he was, it seems, never quite sure of it.

And so one day, as the boys sat by the moat talking things over, the lord's son said, "Jean-Pierre, I saw you off hunting by yourself yesterday! You were after nests?"

"Yes, my little lord."

"You can spot a nest right off in a tree!" (The little lord could never manage to find them quite so easily.) "So did you find any yesterday?"

"Yes, my little lord. I found a good one, full of eggs."

"How many babies were there?"

Jean Pierre held up his hand proudly.

"Ah, five! It *is* a good one. Are they ready yet?"

"No, my little lord. The eggs will not hatch 'til week next."

"Jean-Pierre, tell me, *where* is the nest?"

"Down the path past the spruce trees, in the little fork of the young beech tree."

It was a nest of little blackbirds and they did, in fact, hatch on the sixth day following. It was on the seventh, as Jean-Pierre was on his way to watch over them, that he saw in the distance the young lord stealing away from the woods with the nest in his hands.

He made no attempt to catch him.

What good would it have done to get angry or shout or accuse him?

Instead, Jean-Pierre, kept the lesson in his head so as not to lose it.

Years passed and the boys remained friends, each learning in his own way—the little lord from tutors and books, and Jean-Pierre from his own simple thoughts.

One day as the young men sat by the moat talking things over, the young lord suddenly said to Jean-Pierre, "I watched you go off alone down the road yesterday evening. They say you're courting a beautiful girl."

83

"Yes, my lord, I will not deny she is both fair and dear."

"So, she is really that special?"

"Yes, my lord, and more so."

"So you'll marry her?"

"Yes, my lord."

"And soon?"

"Yes, my lord. I shall ask for her hand week next."

"And may I ask where she lives?"

Jean-Pierre thought a moment, as he always did without haste or concern, and finally said,

"She lives, my lord, down the path past the spruce trees, in the little fork of the beech tree."

PETER FERBER

Finally a careless youth rolled the coin away.

THE HONEST SHILLING

by Hans Christian Andersen

Once long ago there was a silver shilling. He came out quite bright from the Mint, and sprang up and rang out, "Hurrah! Now I'm off into the wide world!" And into the wide world he went. A child held him with soft, warm hands. A miser clutched him in his cold greedy palm. An old man turned him over in his pocket, goodness knows how many times, before parting with him. And, finally, a careless youth rolled him lightly away.

The coin was of good silver, and had very little copper in him. He had been now a whole year in the world, that is to say, in the country in which he had been made. Finally, he landed in the pocket of a travelling man. The gentleman was himself not aware that he still had this coin until he came across it by chance.

"Why here's a shilling from home still left to me," he said fondly. "He shall make the journey with me and remind me of home!"

Denmark lies below Norway and Sweden, and "fans up" above Germany like a feather in a cap.

Abridged and adapted from Andersen's Stories for the Household, Geo. Routledge & Sons, London, 1889 edition.

With that the shilling was thrust back into the man's pocket where it clinked and clanked for joy. It lay happily among different looking companions, as the man had been traveling some time. These came and went, each making room for a successor who always looked different from his predecessor. But the shilling remained safely in the man's pocket for it was special to him.

Several weeks had gone by and the shilling had traveled far out into the world without exactly knowing where he was, though he learned from the other coins that they were called French, Italian, Austrian and Swiss. One said they were from such and such a town, another that he had come to such and such a place. But the shilling couldn't imagine what any of this really meant, for anyone who has his head in a bag sees nothing. And this was the case with the shilling.

But one day he noticed a small opening in the man's pocket and carefully worked his way through it to take a look around (not knowing that you can never get back through a hole you've crept out). He really ought not to have done so, but he was inquisitive, and people often have to pay for that. Nonetheless, he fell to the floor without being seen or heard. Thus the shilling was left behind. Soon, however, he was found and now begins the shilling's life story as told by himself:

"I could hardly believe my ears. The man was saying, 'Away with him, he's no good, of no use!' The words went round and round in my head. I knew I was *silver* and had been properly coined! These people were certainly mistaken! They could not mean me! But, yes, they did mean me.

86

shilling: a coin once used in the United Kingdom worth 12 pence, or 1/20 of a pound.

I, not the other coins, was the one of whom all said, 'He's bad—he's no good at all.'

" 'I must get rid of that fellow in the dark,' said the man who had gotten me last.' And so it went on. Everyone tried to get rid of me, secretly passing me on as a coin of their country.

"What a miserable shilling I was! What use was my silver to me, my value, my coinage, if all these things were looked on as worthless? In the eyes of the world, I could see, you had only the value the world chose to put upon you.

"Every time I was brought out of someone's pocket I shuddered at the thought of the eyes that would look at me, for I knew I would be rejected and tossed off like an imposter or a cheat.

"Once I came into the hands of a poor old woman to whom I was paid for a hard day's work, and she could not get rid of me. No one would accept me, and now I was about to corrupt the old woman's honesty.

" 'I'll have to deceive *someone* with this shilling', she said, 'for even with the best intentions in the world I can't be the one to pay the price for getting a worthless shilling. The rich baker will have to have it! He will be able to bear the loss better than me, but I know it's wrong of me to do it!'

"Now I was not only worthless, but lying heavy on a poor old woman's conscience. 'Is my worth really so different now from the day I was made?' I sighed and asked myself over and over.

"The next day the woman went her way to the rich baker. But he knew too well what I was and threw me back at the woman, who got no bread for me. Now I felt miserable to think I was the cause of so much annoyance

and anger—I who had been in my younger days so proudly conscious of my value and worth.

"The woman was a good woman at heart and took me home with her rather than throwing me away. 'I will not deceive anyone again with this shilling,' I heard her say as we made our way, 'nor let anyone else try to do the same! I will make a hole through it and then put it on a long ribbon and give it to my neighbor's little boy as a medallion!'

"So she bored a hole through me. It is not at all pleasant to have a hole bored through you, I can say, but even the worst things can be borne if the intention is good. And so I became a medal and was hung round the neck of a little child. The child smiled at me and kissed me, and I slept all the night on its warm, innocent neck.

"But when the morning came, the little boy's mother took me up in her bony fingers and had her own thoughts about me. 'This will be mine!' she said in a voice that had no good intentions about it. 'We'll soon see to that!' And she brought out a pair of scissors and cut the ribbon through!

"She put me in vinegar so that I turned a horrible shade of green. Then she plugged up the hole and carried me in the night to a lottery collector and secretly bought a ticket.

"How awful I felt being used like this! The weight of it made me feel that I would crumble to bits. Whether the woman's ticket won anything I'll never know, but this I do know, after that I was sent out into the world to deceive again and again. It was more horrible to bear than anyone can ever know, especially when *I knew* that I was a good coin who was worth something. Of that I was always conscious.

"For a year and a day I thus passed from hand to hand, always abused, always unwelcome. No one trusted me. I lost confidence in the world and in myself. At last, a traveler, a strange gentleman, arrived and I was passed to him. He was polite enough to accept me as good currency, but when he wanted to pass me on again I heard the horrible words, "No good; it's a bad coin!"

" 'But I received it as a good coin,' said the man, as he looked closely at me. Suddenly a smile broke out over his face! I had never seen *that* expression before on any face that looked at me. 'Why, that's one of my own country's coins; a good honest shilling!' said he. 'They call him false and have bored a hole through him! Now this is a curious custom! I must keep him and take him home with me.'

"A feeling of unspeakable joy went through me when I heard myself called a good, honest shilling. And now I was to be taken home, where everyone would know me, and know that I was real and had worth!

"I was wrapped in clean white paper so that I would not be lost again among the other coins and spent. Whenever I was taken out and shown to others they all said how interesting I was. (It is wonderful how interesting you can be without saying a single word.)

"At last I got home again. My joy came back to me for I was of good silver and had the right stamp and did no longer suffer even though a hole had been bored through me, as through a false coin. But that doesn't matter if you are not really false. You must wait for the end, and you will be righted at last, that's what I truly believe," said the honest shilling.

89

This special story takes on even more meaning knowing something of Andersen's life. The story is more fact than fiction, and wholly autobiographical as are most of his stories, including The Ugly Duckling.

At fourteen, Andersen left home for Copenhagen, determined to make something of himself. Physically homely and often thought "odd," if talented, it would take many years of hard work, disappointment, and determination before he would return home to Odense, Denmark, an author whose "value" was recognized not only in his own country, but the world over.

The wolf will dwell with the lamb,
and the leopard will lie down with
the kid; and the calf and the
young lion will grow up together;
and a little child will
lead them.

⌘
ISAIAH

Journey II

TO THE PEACEABLE KINGDOM

Your second journey will take you to a
kingdom where animals have learned to
speak and live together in peace. It is up
to you to discover what they did *not* learn.

A DINOSAUR'S TALE

by Priscilla Harper

HERE WAS A time when the earth possessed itself—when *mine* and *yours* were unknown. It was a time when continents had no names; countries and borders did not exist, and cities, towns, and villages were not even a thought. This was the time of the mighty dinosaur: a magnificent period in the earth's history called the *Cretaceous*. This was the reign of *Tyrannosaurus rex*. Listen to her and she will take you back to her world—to a world before ours, a world before borders, a world so very different and, in some ways, much the same:

"I am a mighty creature, a giant from the past, a marvel to your eyes. I am *Tyrannosaurus SUE*. Stand by my side, and you will barely reach my knee. Stand near as I walk, and you will feel the earth tremble! Look high above you into my cavernous mouth. To you it will appear as a cave to lie down in. I am quick and I am powerful. My size is surpassed only by my

In 1990 the most complete T.rex ever found was discovered by field paleontologist, Sue Hendrickson, in the badlands of South Dakota. The T.rex was eventually named SUE in her honor. Her skull is five feet long and weighs 600 pounds.

strength. With my tail balanced behind me, I move in quick, swift strides. My thick, muscular legs give power to my massive frame. Stand in awe of my might, but see also my majesty!

"Enter my world and you will find that your favorite furry friends—the cat and the dog—are not here yet. Neither are there creatures with hair —horses, or goats, or deer. The crocodile and fish, and turtles and lizards and birds and insects, are all that will be familiar to you. Flowers have recently arrived, adding their vibrant colors to a world of green. The wasps are here sipping their sweet nectar, and the intimate relationship between insect and flower has begun. Soon the butterfly will join our world.

"Now listen to the *sounds* of my world. Leave your words behind, for they will fall silent here! They won't be understood. The flying *Pterosaurs*, endlessly circling the globe, crying out with their haunting, beckoning call and their loud clacking beaks are beginning at last to surrender the skies to the birds. From morning until evening you will hear their ever-present chorus. You will hear the call of my kin echoing throughout the lush forest, and the plaintive call of our young asking for food. You will hear the deep baritone voice of the armored *Ankylosaurus* making its solemn presence known—its great club tail sweeping across the earth. Deep trumpeting sounds, high rasping sounds, steady humming sounds, burrowing sounds, pounding sounds—these are all the voices of the *Cretaceous*!

"My world is a world of wondrous sound! Listen! You will hear the sound of the rhythmic beat of a rainstorm, and of a single droplet of water parting from the tip of a fern. You will hear the sound of the wind dancing through the trees, and the river bed cracking and parting during the dry season. All is sound here—but no words. You will hear the grinding sound of vegetation being eaten by the swift *duckbills*—their herd of thousands moving in one accord to create a great stampeding sound. You will hear the loud felling of trees as the dinosaurs make their way through the thick forest. Everywhere there is sound!

94

"The end of the great *Cretaceous* period is near. The continents are taking on forms now familiar to you. I have lived a long life. As I take to my resting place by the edge of a flowing river, I know I will be seen again. I will not be forgotten. The earth will not let the age of the mighty dinosaur be forgotten. . . .

δ

"For 65 million years I have lain silent in the earth, but never still. I have slept in smooth, solid lands that turned to jagged cliffs. Rivers dried up all around me and valleys formed. Lands separated, shifted, folded, and buckled—and, yet, I waited to be discovered.

"Then came the time when I could no longer stay silent nor remain unseen—left embedded meaninglessly within deep rocks and crevices. I cracked the earth! I called out to be found . . . and one person heard! I cannot tell you how, only that she *knew* the treasures so faithfully wrapped and hidden away by the earth were here, preserved, waiting to be found.

"She listened, but not with her ears. She walked the earth, but not with uncaring step to my sandstone cliff. She saw, but with more than her eyes. She brought me out, and now I stand as a testament to a time long ago, a time when the earth possessed itself, a time not meant to be forgotten. . . ."

WAKING TYRANNOSAURUS SUE

by Sue Hendrickson

I LOOK FOR dinosaurs for a living. At least, that's *part* of what I do. Dinosaurs are normally very hard to find, especially a *Tyrannosaurus rex*, because there were not as many of them as other kinds of dinosaurs. Even if there had been, it can be hard to find your notebook or tennis shoes in your own room, let alone the remains of something that has lain buried in the earth for millions and millions of years. Still, I always expected that someday, if I was patient and persistent enough, I might find one—at least *part* of one: an elbow or a little toe, or perhaps a rib. I never dreamed, however, that a dinosaur would find me. . . .

It happened in August, back in 1990, in the badlands of South Dakota. It's hot in the badlands in August—REALLY HOT—and that doesn't make finding a dinosaur any easier. I had been there for several weeks looking for dinosaur remains with a team of field paleontologists. The team was

In 1990 field paleontologist Sue Hendrickson discovered the most complete T. rex ever found. The magnificent creature is now permanently on display at Chicago's Field Museum of Natural History.

Peter, Terry, Matt (who was ten years old), Jason (who was fifteen), and Gypsy—my golden retriever. And me, Sue.

We camped out six weeks that summer, rising early every morning with the sunrise, quickly eating, and then setting out for the fossil search. To find dinosaur bones, you have to walk . . . and walk . . . and walk, patiently searching, and carefully looking, where there are no trees or plants or grass that might cover up the bones. So the best place to look is in desert terrain, like the badlands.

Matt often went looking in the same direction I did. He found all kinds of *T. rex* teeth that summer! (It might be a record, because he found over twenty teeth.) I kept telling Matt it was great that he found yet another tooth, but I was looking for the whole thing! Of course, I was joking. It's nearly impossible to find a complete dinosaur of any kind—let alone a *T. rex*.

In this part of South Dakota, we were looking for dinosaurs of the Cretaceous period—the last time period when the dinosaurs roamed the earth. Often we found scraps of bones from duck-billed dinosaurs (called *hadrosaurs*) and *Triceratops*, but rarely a complete bone. It was just mostly pieces. Matt found a *Triceratops* skull that was about 30% complete, which is very good! So we spent quite a few days digging and extracting these bones from the ground.

We were looking in this area for more than two weeks, and from the very beginning I had a strange feeling. It's almost impossible to describe, but I knew I shouldn't ignore it. It was more than a feeling. Or, if it was just a feeling it was pulling me like a magnet to a spot we had missed. One

96

Cretaceous: The time period lasting from about 136 million to about 65 million years ago. The name alludes to the abundance of chalk that was formed then. (In Latin the word for chalk is creta.) At the beginning of this period, all the continents had been joined as one land mass, called Pangaea. The breakup of Pangaea created what are now our continents.

day when I was on top of a ridge—looking back across the valley where we had already looked—I suddenly saw a small outcrop that we had missed. I counted seven rock exposures and we had only looked at six. Somehow I knew that that one last area was waiting just for me. I *had* to get to it.

The problem was, there was no time to go explore it. We were trying to finish the *Triceratops's* skull so we could go home. After weeks in a hot, dry desert, our blue jeans needed washing pretty badly—and, even more, we were really looking forward to a hot shower and to sleeping in a bed again. Still, I couldn't stop thinking about that seventh rock exposure. I knew I *had* to go there! But how? There were only two days left now, and we still had so much to do. We had to finish digging up the *Triceratops*, and then there were hundreds of bones to pack up before we could get started on breaking up our campsite.

When we woke up the last morning, to our frustration, we discovered that not only was there a flat tire on the truck, but the spare was so low we couldn't drive to the dig site. I told Matt and Jason and Pete and Terry, "While you go to town to fix the tires, this will finally give me a chance to look at that ledge that's been calling me for two weeks."

So Gypsy and I set off on foot across the valley. It was a *long* way across the valley. What made things even worse, was that a heavy fog was covering everything. That never happens in the desert in the summer. It was as if it was trying to keep me from my goal, but I was determined not to let it. Gypsy and I started out even though we couldn't see where we were going. I told myself not to walk in a circle, and I told Gypsy not to let us either. We were both good navigators so I was amazed when two hours later we ended up back at the camp! Already it felt like it had been a long day. But I had to get there. We started again. Finally, after four more hours of hard going we made it to the seventh rock ledge.

I started walking slowly along the bottom of the cliff face, looking very carefully. I was scanning the ground for bones, trying hard not to be tricked by all the shards of rock and clumps of earth, and trying very hard not to miss anything.

98

And then it happened. There they were . . . pieces of dinosaur bones on the ground! When I spotted them I looked up immediately, and there, eight feet above me I could see whole bones sticking out of the rock. I carefully climbed up on the ledge to look more closely—making sure not to step on the bones. Instantly my brain started to work deciphering what I was seeing. There were vertebrae (or backbones). Then another end of a bone . . . a rib! And then a big bone partly fallen down the hill—but it was too deteriorated to identify. And then, best of all, bones that continued into the hill at both ends. That meant that hopefully more would be found.

The bones were very different from those of the *duckbill* and *Triceratops* that we were so used to finding. These were hollow (like a chicken's, or a bird's) so I knew it had to be a meat-eating dinosaur. Even more, the back bones were *huge*, so I was sure they must belong to a *T. rex*.

At that time only eleven T. rexes had ever been found.

"Gypsy!" I called out excitedly, "It must be a *T. rex*. But it *can't* be a *T. rex*. Nobody finds a *T. rex!*" But it *was* a T. rex.

Can you imagine how excited I was? I was looking at the largest meat-eating dinosaur that had ever lived. Even more, I was looking at a creature that had lived 65 million years ago and was here waiting to be found!

But that's when I realized the dinosaur had found me.

Just think, she had waited millions and millions of years for the right moment to reveal herself to the human race, and for a human who knew what her bones meant. She had waited all these centuries to make herself known even though she had no way to speak—to make someone feel her in the earth. And that someone was me. I could hardly believe that she had found *me*. And it's still hard to believe.

She was just beginning to come out of the rock. Now was the time she had to make herself known. The more she was exposed—without being found—the more she would erode until only the last piece of the last bone would be left, which is what almost always happens. But it didn't happen this time. After millions of years I was the one who heard her calling out —calling to be dug up, so that everyone on earth would come to know her and learn about her world—*our own world*.

δ

I couldn't wait to tell the others! Gypsy and I ran back to the site where we found the rest of the team on their hands and knees excavating the last of the *Triceratops's* skull. When I carefully held out the two pieces of broken bone I had brought back with me, Pete was amazed: a *T. rex*—and more than one bone. (It's very rare to find more than one bone.) Everyone wanted to go to the site right away, but I asked Pete to come alone with Gypsy and me. It was a very special moment, you see. I gave him the gift of every dinosaur hunter's dreams: a *T. rex*.

When we got there, Pete actually jumped up and down; that was how excited he was. Then he said, "It's all there! I just know it's all there!" That night at the campsite, Terry and Pete decided to name the dinosaur *T. rex* "SUE" after me.

100

It took us many days to dig the rock away just to get to the bone layer —and then many more days to uncover all of the bones. Day after day we worked. After several days, we had found nearly every bone except the head. Pete finally gave up hope of finding it and started to dig down the side of the pelvis to get it ready to take out of the ground when . . . guess what he found? The WHOLE skull—with TEETH! We couldn't believe how beautiful it was, or how beautifully it was preserved. It was as if the earth had been determined that this amazing creature would not be forgotten, no matter how long she had to wait to be found.

Matt was jealous for a few days because I had broken his record on the number of teeth found. Yet the more we uncovered *T. rex SUE*, and the more we thought about how amazing it was that she had lived and walked this earth, right where we were now walking, we lost our silly human emotions. Instead, we all worked together in complete awe of her, eager to let her come back to the living world.

I'll always be grateful I was found by a dinosaur. I like to think it happened because of my respect for her, and respect for this world of ours. It's lasted such a long time, and has so much to tell us. Imagine all the things waiting to show themselves to us! There's a whole world of them, in fact. Who knows, maybe there's a dinosaur waiting for you.

SMALL CREATURES

An old Turkish tale
as retold by Diane Cihangir

A RABBIT hopped out of his burrow one morning to get a bite to eat. While munching the sweet grass covering his little hidden house, he suddenly heard a wolf call out, "I'm going to eat you!"

The rabbit was very frightened but managed to think quickly enough to say, "Oh no, Brother Wolf, you won't be able to do that!" Then he pointed behind the wolf and continued, "If anyone is going to eat me, it will be that hunter there who is about to kill you!"

Greatly fearing hunters, the wolf looked behind him to see if there was really a hunter there—and quick as a flash the little rabbit scurried back into his burrow!

Let this be a lesson to you. Don't look down on little things. They may be far wiser than you!

YELLOW FOX

102

An old Pawnee Tale
by George Bird Grinnell

George Bird Grinnell is credited with having done more than any other person to preserve the cultural history of the Plains Indians. For more than forty years, he spent each summer with various tribes learning their language, history, culture, and folktales.

HILE THE Pawnees were on their winter hunt, a young boy whose name was *Kiwuk-u lah'-kahta* (Yellow Fox) went out alone to see if he could kill a deer. When he left the campsite in the morning it was warm and pleasant, but in the middle of the day a great storm of wind and snow came, and the flying snow hid everything and it grew very cold. By and by, the ground covered with snow and the whole look of the prairie was changed. The boy became lost and did not know where he was, nor which way to go to get to the camp.

All day he walked—but he saw nothing of the camp, nor of any trail. As it became colder and colder, he thought that he would surely freeze to death. He thought that he must die and that there was no hope of his ever seeing his people again.

As he was wandering along, numbed and stiffened by the cold and

*The conquering of difficulties is
one of the chief joys of life.*

GEORGE BIRD GRINNELL

103

stumbling through the deep snow, he heard behind him a curious singing sound, and in time with the singing was the noise made by some heavy animal, running. The sounds came nearer and nearer, and at last, close by the boy, ran a great buffalo bull. As he ran near the boy he sang a song, and, as he sang, the sound of his hoofs on the ground kept time to the measure of the song.

This is what he sang:

A-ti-us ti-wa-ko Ru-ru!	My Father says, Go on!
Teh-wah-hwa'-ko Ru-ru-hwa'-hwa'	He keeps saying, keep going on!
Wi-ruh-ree	It will be well.

The boy's heart became strong when he heard the Father had sent the bull, and he followed him, and the bull led him home.

When Indians wanted to signal to each other the approach of a Pawnee, they would make the sign for wolf by making a fist and extending two fingers like a wolf's ears.

Pawnees were known for their ability to sneak into their enemy's camp. The name was also given to them because of their amazing endurance.

Grinnell's diaries recorded their ability to travel all day and dance all night. It was not unusual for a Pawnee warrior to be able to run 100 miles in twenty-four hours.

The rooster made the most noise.

BEAU BEAR AND OTHER STORIES

Stories from an Adirondack farm
by Gramma Droegemueller

AN AND TOM lived on a big farm in the foothills of the Adirondacks. They *loved* animals, and so enjoyed going to farm auctions and buying whatever animals were not wanted. One day they brought home three Rhode Island Red chickens, two hens and a rooster. Like most chickens, they were free to roam about the farm.

The rooster made the most noise, of course, and acted like a watchdog—but it was one little hen who was the boss, and she followed Tom wherever he went.

One day, at another auction, Tom and Jan bought some baby ducklings. The babies had to be kept warm, and so Tom built an incubator for them and set it up on the back porch. Little hen, or Tic Tac as Tom called her, claimed the babies as her very own and hovered over the box where they

were kept as faithfully as if she were a mother duck.

Each morning Tom would go out to feed them and put clean paper in their pen, and always Tic Tac was right there to supervise. One morning after Tom removed the heater and started to clean the box, his telephone rang and he left to answer it. It was a neighbor with some news and so Tom got to talking and forgot all about the chore he hadn't finished.

Suddenly Tic Tac appeared at the glass door clucking and fussing and fluttering her wings. Tom shooed her away, but in a few minutes she was back. This time she pecked at the window and clucked loudly. Tom shooed her away again but she refused to go! So Tom said goodbye to his neighbor and went back out on the porch—only to discover a fire beside the ducklings' box! Tom had left the electric heater sitting on top of the pile of newspapers and they had caught on fire. Tom looked admiringly at Tic Tac as Tic Tac looked on proudly having saved her ducklings and Tom's house from burning!

Then there was the amazing experience Tom had with Beau Bear the day he was cutting hay in the field across the road from the house. Beau Bear was a big black dog Tom found at his door one morning. He was hungry and very friendly. Tom advertised in the local paper, but no one claimed him so he named him Beau Bear (*Beautiful Bear*) and they became inseparable. Beau Bear was always at Tom's side so when Tom took the tractor out to cut hay, Beau Bear, of course, was there too. However, when Tom got to the middle of the field, Beau Bear ran in front of the tractor barking madly and refusing to move. The tractor got closer and closer. Finally Tom got off to see if something was wrong with Beau Bear only to discover a tiny fawn lying in the tall grass. She was perfectly healthy, but newborn. Tom knew he shouldn't touch her or the mother would smell the human scent and go away.

107

Tom postponed the haying while Beau Bear guarded the field until Tom finally called him home. The mother deer moved her fawn away and the next day Tom and Beau Bear finished cutting the hay.

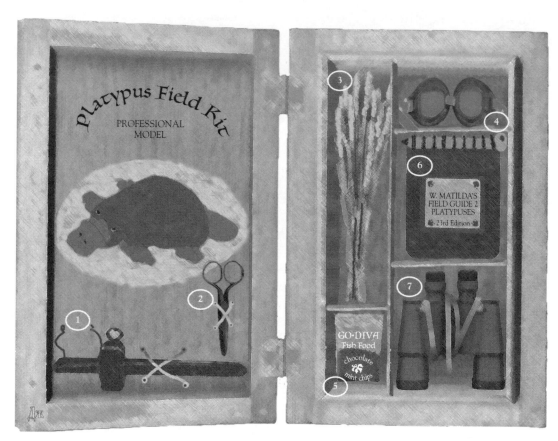

1	**C. Little's Egg Sizemometer.** Sizes: small, medium, and jumbo. Felt-lined clip for maximum egg comfort.
2	**Shear Delight Fur Sampling System.** Features include: non-tickling tips; built-in CD player to entertain platypuses while you snip away.
3	**All Natural Camoflage Grasses.** Come within inches of the shyest platypus! Waterproofed with plenty of airflow.

4	**DownUnder Face Mask.** For underwater observation. Colors: coral or seaweed.
5	**Go-Diva Fish Treats.** Should a platypus get wind that you're following him, surround yourself with fish by giving them Go-Diva mint chocolate chips.
6	**W. Matilda's Field Guide 2 Platypuses.** Includes matching designer pencil.
7	**Platyzoom Field Glasses.** Eye-pieces (wide end) double as miniture fry pans.

IF YOU ASK A PLATYPUS

An Aboriginal tale from New South Wales
as retold by Pauline E. McLeod

ONG, LONG AGO when the world was very young, all the creatures of the earth began to argue and ARGUE and ARGUE over who was most important!

To settle the question once and for all, the Animal Creatures held a meeting and unanimously voted that *they* were the most important of all the creatures on earth! After all, Animals have soft, lovely fur and can run swiftly over the land. But to make it *absolutely clear* to everyone else, the Animals agree that there should be a Special Group that only Animals could join.

Then someone piped up and said: "What about the Platypus? He is, of course, a little different from the rest of us, but he does have fur and he runs across the land. Certainly the Platypus should be asked to join The Special Group that only Animals can join!"

Pauline E. McLeod is a young Aboriginal story teller who has been telling Dreaming *stories for over ten years now. The stories of Dreamtime—the period, according to Aboriginal folklore, when the world came into being—have been handed down from generation to generation for thousands of years as an oral tradition. Within the stories are lessons on behavior and customs, including respect for all the creatures of earth. These stories are a very important part of Aboriginal culture.*

Everyone agreed and ran off to ask the Platypus if he would like to join The Special Group that only Animals could join.

The Platypus, who is a very shy creature, listened to what the Animals had to say and then replied, "Thank you very much for asking me to join your Special Group! I am sure it is a great honor, but I will have to think about it, and in a few days I will let you know what I have decided."

Meanwhile, it seems that all the Birds were holding their own meeting at which they unanimously agreed that *they* were the most important of all the creatures on earth. After all, as everyone could see, unlike any other creature, Birds have gorgeous feathers and can fly high above the earth. Nevertheless, to make it *absolutely clear* to everyone else, the Birds agreed that there should be a Special Group that only Birds could join.

Then someone piped up and said "The Emu can't fly! How can he be a bird?"

With that, the Emu squawked indignantly, "Why I am the fastest running bird of all! I could beat any one of you in a foot race! Besides, my wife lays eggs which is proof that we are certainly Birds!"

This, everyone had to agree with, of course, and so they told the Emu he could join The Special Group that only Birds could join.

No sooner had the Emu smoothed his ruffled feathers when someone else piped up and said, "What about the Platypus? We all know he's a little different from the rest of us, but he does have a bill and his wife lays eggs. So, to be absolutely fair, the Platypus should be asked to join The Special Group that only Birds can join."

All the Birds agreed and quickly flew off (except the Emu, who ran) to where the Platypus lived to ask if he would join their Special Group.

The Platypus, being a very shy creature, listened politely to what the Birds had to say and then replied most modestly, "Thank you very much for asking! I am sure it is a very great honor—but I really will have to think about it and let you know in a few days what I have decided."

Meanwhile, on the very same day right next door to where the Platypus lived, all the Water Creatures were holding a meeting at which they, too, voted that *they* were the most important of all the creatures on earth.

"After all," they spurted, sputtered, and spouted to one another, "anyone can see that there is far more water than land on earth, which certainly proves that the Water Creatures are the most special of all."

And, of course, all the Water Creatures agreed.

But then someone piped up and said, "What about the Platypus? We all know he's a little different from the rest of us, but his home is right on the water's edge—and there's no denying that he swims and explores the underwater world as happily as the rest of us. So, to be fair, the Platypus really should be asked to be a part of The Special Group that only Water Creatures can join!"

All the Water Creatures agreed and so swam to the water's edge to ask the Platypus if he would like to join their Special Group.

The Platypus, being very shy, was so surprised at yet a third invitation in one day that he almost fainted! When he recovered himself, he managed to say, "Thank you very much. I'm sure it is a great honor, but my poor head needs a rest before it can decide such an important matter."

The poor Platypus had thought far more thoughts than he normally did

111

in one day, and so he decided the best thing would be to ask his family what they thought. Which Special Group was The Most Special Group of All The Special Groups to join?

The Animals? The Birds? Or the Water Creatures?

Mother Platypus began by saying, "I think we should join the Birds. After all, we have distinguished bills and I'm the one who lays the eggs!"

But then the Platypus's pretty daughter piped up and said, "I think we should join the Animals because we have *beautiful fur.*"

But no sooner had she said this when his son complained, "No, Dad! Think how much we love to swim and explore underwater! Please, please join the Water Creatures!"

Father Platypus shook his head and said, "No good . . . it's no good! We can't join all three groups! We can only join one!"

"Well," consoled Mother Platypus, trying to be helpful, "Why don't you go for a little walk and think about it again."

So the Platypus went for a walk, and while he was walking and trying to think, and thinking and trying to walk, he came upon his cousin, the Echidna. "Well, well," thought the Platypus, "this is a very good thing for the Echidna is a rather strange creature, too, and he will know what Group is best for me to join." (In case you've forgotten, the Echidna is the creature that came with spikes.)

"Good day, Cousin Echidna!" said the Platypus pleasantly. "Everyone's talking about joining Groups these days! Whose Group do you think I should join?"

"Well," answered the Echidna, "I wouldn't join any Group if I were you!

You're sure to get into trouble with one or the other of them, so if I were you I wouldn't join any at all!"

"That's no good," moaned the Platypus. "I've got to join someone's Group. You can't not belong to a *Group*!" So the Platypus politely said goodbye, promising to let the Echidna know what he finally decided.

113

Days and days went by and still the Platypus couldn't decide. Finally, he had an idea!

He would call a meeting of all the Animals, and all the Birds, and all the Water Creatures (which was a very brave thing to do for, as you know, the Platypus is a very shy creature) and make an Announcement.

No sooner had all the creatures gathered, than they began to argue amongst themselves over whose Special Group the Platypus would want to join. In fact, they were arguing so loudly that the poor Platypus could hardly bring himself to come out. Finally, he struck up his courage and, climbing onto a log, cleared his voice and said, "Excuse me! Hello there! Excuse me! Thank you all for coming here today. I would just like to say. . . .Well, you see, I would just like to say, that I have decided not to join any group whatsoever!"

"What!" cried all the Animals, the Birds and the Water Creatures in amazement. "That's impossible! You *have* to join someone's Group!"

"Please! Oh, please! Do listen to me," pleaded the Platypus. "What I meant to say is, don't you see, you don't have to join anyone's Special Group to be special. As you've said already, I'm a little different from all

of you and I'm a little bit the same. And I would just like to add that I'm special in my own special way! I happen to be a little bit Animal, a little bit Bird, and a little bit Water Creature. But I think if you looked carefully, each of you would find that we are all a little bit the same, but we are still all special in our own special way. I can't say for sure why we're not all the same. But as long as we're different there's no need to go around making Groups out of it! If you stop to think about it, it's really rather nice that we're all unique and that everyone doesn't look like me!"

114

The Animals all laughed at the thought of having bills, and the Birds all laughed at the thought of not having feathers, and everyone knew the Water Creatures were laughing because all over the surface of the water bubbles suddenly appeared!

The Platypus was quite sure there was nothing else he needed to say and so stepped down from his log.

And then the most amazing thing happened. The Animals, the Birds, and the Water Creatures all stopped arguing. "Why, yes, we're all special in our own special way!" they were laughing and saying to one another. And everyone agreed that the Platypus was very wise indeed!

And that is why our ancestors—the Aboriginal peoples—have never hunted the Platypus. For he reminds us that we, too, are special in our own special way!

FRIEND BUTTERFLY

A little Rwandan children's song
Shared and translated into English from Kinyarwanda
by Louise Mushikiwabo

AYINGILIYE APOLLINARIE

AKANYUGUNYUGU

Dore akanyugunyugu k'amabara meza!
Icyampa ngo kaze nkagire
inshuti. Nakigisha kubara,
Gusoma no kwandilka
Nk'uko mwalimu
yabitwigishije.

FRIEND BUTTERFLY

Oh what a butterfly with beautiful colors!
I wish she'd come here and
be my best friend. I'd teach
her how to count and read
and write, the way our
teacher taught us.

In Rwanda
it is said that there is a song for
everything: for getting up in the morning and
going to bed, for running, skipping, laughing, and
playing — and especially for learning,
the most important thing of all.

Here you will stay and turn into monkeys!

HOW MONKEYS CAME TO BE

An old Belize tale as retold
by Rachel Crandell

THIS
very hot evening Eladio Pop
is sitting in the shade of the calabash tree with his
ten children all gathered close around him. They are sitting on
the top of a hill, catching whatever breeze they can. Their father, you
see, is about to tell them the *wonderful story* of how monkeys came to be:

calabash tree:
a gourd tree

118

lianas: a general term for woody vines and includes the monkey ladder vine.

"My father tell me this story. It start with the Sun and the Moon. They are the first generation; that is how the Mayas believe. They have children. I think 15 children. They tell the children, 'Go into the forest, go on and work a little; make a clearing. Clear for the corn. Take your tools for cutting and digging and planting.'

"So these children they go. I don't know how far, maybe close by like the forest is here to us. The children went and the Mother, the Moon, she stay home. The Sun and the Moon, the Father and the Mother, know the spot where the children be working. They leave them alone. They just tell them, 'Go.'

"So the children they be gone, all by themselves. They come to where they must be working. But they see the beautiful trees . . . they see the beautiful *lianas* . . . they are kids . . . they start to play! They go from tree to tree; they swing high on the beautiful *lianas*. They don't even know when the day pass by! They keep playing, and so the evening come. They say, 'O.K.! Let us go back.'

"They come home and the Sun and the Moon, they ask, 'How is it you come back? Are you doing a lot of work today?'

"And the kids they say, 'Yes, we did some work.'

" 'O.K., are you sure?' ask the Sun and the Moon.

" 'Oh, yes!'

"The next day they go to the same spot to start to chop. The Mother have in mind that they work. But the forest, it be SO beautiful! They climb on the beautiful *lianas*. The day it goes. For five days it goes like this. So now their Mother, the Moon, she wants to see what kind of work they are doing. She reach the place, but there is *no work!* She reach the spot but there is *nothing!* She say, 'Where are these kids?" Ah, these kids they are quiet. They know someone is coming! The Mother take a deep look. These kids they are in the trees!

" 'Oh,' say the Moon, 'is that the work I told you to do?'

"Everybody quiet.

" 'Yes, where is the work?'

"Everybody quiet.

" 'O.K.,' the Moon say, 'so this is what you are doing here? It look to me like you disobey! It look to me like you love to play!! It look to me like here you will stay and turn into monkeys!!!'

"They stay there for always, 'til right now. They are the first generation of monkey. That is how the monkey come! And he still is playing!"

O

NCE

again the hot sun was
ready to set. Eladio's children were smiling.
They jumped up quickly and ran away like naughty
little howler monkeys banished to the treetops forever!

She lived in a little cottage with a garden.

THE CONVIVIAL GUEST

Adapted from the French tale by Henri Pourrat

KIND SHE WAS, though poor, and now a widow. She lived in a little cottage with a garden, and every summer she went to the fair in Ambert, which was where she bought a little nanny-goat to keep her company, and give her a cup of milk now and then. On her way home, she met neighbor Gruyère.

"*Naturellement*," she replied to neighbor Gruyère "I know what I'm doing! A little goat to keep me company and give me a cup of milk."

naturellement: naturally

"But where will you keep her?" asked neighbor Gruyère in alarm.

"Well, in warm weather I'll let her be in the yard. . ."

"But what will you do with her in the *winter?*"

"Heavens, in the winter I'll keep her in my little cottage."

"But a goat—what about *l'odeur?!*" gasped neighbor Gruyère.

"*L'odeur?* Well, what can I do? The poor thing will just have to get used to it!"

l'odeur: the odor

Hywel squeezed himself under the kitchen table.

HYWEL AND GWYDDEL

An old Welsh tale collected with the kind help
of Nicola Jones and the children of Ysgol Garth Olwg

BRAG, BRAG, BRAG, BRAG! That was all Hywel did from the first light of the morning sun, till the silvery moon hung low in the evening sky. With Hywel bellowing at the top of his lungs day and night, and night and day, and so on . . . there was not a moment's peace in Rhondda Valley. Everyone who lived in the valley was fed up with him! But what was one to do? After all, Hywel was a giant, and even though everyone knows that giants are just big babies, do *you* know anyone willing to get on the wrong side of anyone that big—even if he is a baby? And so everyone simply put up with his boring old chant:

FI YW'R MWYAF!
FI YW'R GORAU!
FI YW'R GORAU YN Y BYD MAWR I GYD!

Wales is a gentle and generous land within the United Kingdom. Nearly the whole of Pontypridd helped to find this story for you! First a woman named Priscilla phoned her friend Naomi, who phoned her grandparents the VanTilborgs, who phoned Nicola, whose son Ben, and his friends, along with the headmaster of Ysgol Garth Olwg, Mr. R.E. Hughes, all agreed this story would delight you!

I am the biggest!
I am the best!
I am the greatest in the whole world!

Even big babies have to grow up some time, however, and here's how Hywel grew up.

Everyone knew (but no one ever said it aloud in front of Hywel) that the **BIGGEST** giant in all the world lived in Ireland. He terrified the whole of the island, and would have terrified the whole world if he had known how to swim, but he didn't. Thus he stuck to terrifying the poor people of Ireland.

One day Hywel, knowing that Gwyddel (that was the big Irish giant's name) lived far across the sea, with all that water lying in between, challenged Gwyddel to a first-rate *arfod*. What Hywel didn't know, however, was that Gwyddel was big enough, and strong enough, to jump right over the Irish Sea—Cardigan Bay and all—in one big leap. If he pushed off with his left foot in Dublin, he could put his right foot down K'BOOM! on the whole of Pontypridd before you could say, *Fi yw'r gorau!*

And so Hywel kept up his boasting day and night, until even Hywel's dog could stand it no more and left to live with a neighbor—while his wife took to wearing the cat on her head like ear-muffs. Finally, one day, as Hywel was sitting outside waiting for his wife to serve him breakfast, what should he see in the distance but a HUGE SHAPE, moving slowly towards him. Gywddel was so big, in fact, that he looked like a giant glacier moving through the Rhondda Valley. Hywel fled into the house in terror, past his wife, and quick as a flash squeezed himself under the kitchen table.

"What on earth are you doin' waitin' for your breakfast under the table, Hywel!" said his wife in surprise.

"I'm *not* waitin' for breakfast under the table, wife!" bellowed Hywel,

124

arfod: fight, battle.

I'm the best!

his heart pounding like a clock and his legs quivering like jellies. "Can't you see IT'S THE GIANT FROM IRELAND come after me!"

"I thought you said he couldn't swim!"

"He doesn't need to! Just take a look out the window. Oh my! Oh my! Whatever shall I do?" said Hywel shaking now like an earthquake.

"Don't worry, Hywel," said his wife calmly. "I'll save you! Just do what I tell you! Quick, get yourself upstairs and hide under the bed!"

"Wife, that's no idea! Everyone knows that everyone hides under the bed! He's sure to find me there."

"Do as I tell you if you value your life! You really are a very silly giant, Hywel, getting yourself into such a mess."

"You're right, you're right, wife! But if you save my life, I promise I'll never brag again," snivelled Hywel pathetically. . .

They could now smell Gywddel's breath outside the door.

"Cross-your-heart? Honest-to-goodness?" asked the wife gleefully. (She was, after all, tired of being told how lucky she was to be Hywel's wife.)

"Yes, yes!" cried Hywel fleeing up the stairs.

"Wait!" yelled the wife. "Give me your shoes."

Two shoes thudded to the floor, and no sooner had the wife put them in front of the fireplace, than Gwyddel's head appeared in the door.

"Top of the mornin' to you! Is there a welcome here for Gwyddel, an extraordinary giant from Ireland?" chuckled a booming Irish voice.

"Well, of course, any giant from Ireland is welcome at our table! Do come in, Gwyddel. You're just in time for breakfast. As soon as Hywel comes home you'll be our guest!"

"Aye," said Gwyddel, "He'll be the giant I've come all this way to see. And where would he be then? Hiding under the bed, perhaps?" laughed Gwyddel as he pointed at the two enormous shoes sitting in front of the fire. "I don't expect that Hywel usually goes visiting in bare feet, does he now?"

"No, indeed!" said the wife indignantly. "Why haven't you ever seen a *bach's* shoes before? Those be the *bach's* shoes! My *cariad bach* is still asleep upstairs in his cot."

Gwyddel looked again at the shoes. . .

Gwyddel began to think. . .

Then said Gwyddel to himself, "*Connemara!* If those be the *bach's* shoes, his Daddy must be ENORMOUS!

"Errr, Missus," said Gwyddel flubbering and blubbering like all giants do who are really just big babies, "I've just remembered some urgent, some *very urgent, important* business I've to see to in Tipperary! Tell your Hywel how sorry I was to miss him. . . ."

When Gwyddel was back in Ireland, Hywel finally came out from under the bed. From that day on he never boasted again—not, however, that he didn't *want* to. But his wife had threatened to tell everyone how she had saved him from the terrifying giant of Ireland if he did.

126

bach: baby

cariad bach: my beloved babe

Connemara: a very beautiful area in western Ireland.

ISOMASHII, LORD OF THE RICE BAG

Abridged and adapted from an old Japanese tale

SOMASHII was a soldier and had spent all his life defending the Emperor's kingdom against wild beasts and attacking enemies. As a result, he knew all of their tricks and had long since ceased to be afraid of them. However, hard times had fallen on the land and he and his wife and little child were often hungry. Each day Isomashii watched the rice bag grow smaller and smaller, and for the first time since he could remember he became afraid.

One day, as Isomashii stood guarding a gate, a snake appeared waiting, ready to strike. Without a word, Isomashii brought his strong boot down upon the snake's head. Instantly the snake was gone and a wise old man stood where the snake had been and laughed heartily. Isomashii thought he must have been dreaming! But when it was time to for him to return home, suddenly a dragon appeared at the edge of the forest. Without a word, Isomashii spit on the head of an arrow and sent it flying into the beast's terrible head. Instantly the dragon was gone and, again, a wise old man stood where the dragon had been, laughing. Amazed at his strange day, Isomashii headed for home wondering what it all meant.

No sooner had Isomashii opened the door when his eye caught sight of the empty rice bag. Without a word Isomashii grabbed the bag and spit on it and then laughed heartily. From that day on he was not afraid and the rice bag always contained enough for his family and their friends

127

Isomashii: brave, valiant, or gallant one.

There is a Japanese proverb which says, "If you spit on an arrow, it will kill any creature no matter how large or terrible." It means: if you disdain an enemy you will defeat him.

PETER FERBER

*The faithful perro and the gentle pescador shared the work,
weathered together under the hot ocean sun, and journeyed home to share the
same meal, the same fire, and to sleep side by side.*

THE PERRO

An old Puerto Rican legend of the famous San Juan coral
Collected with the kind help of Celeste Breslow

ISLANDERS CALLED IT BORINQUEN, for it was like a paradise to them. That was long ago, when the Spanish conquistadors ruled the brilliant blue seas of the coveted Antilles, and unfurled their proud flag from the north turret of El Morro. The Spaniards, however, called it *San Juan Bautista Puerto Rico*: the rich port of St. John the Baptist, because in those days it was the possession of the church which belonged to their Spanish Queen.

Still, for the islanders, it was *Borinquen*—where life was lived in *gentleness*. Here, in a small room along the narrowest of streets of San Juan Bautista, lived the *perro* who, with a gentle *pescador*, went daily to the sea —for they were fishers.

perro: dog.
pescador: fisherman.

Early each day, for more years than the faithful *perro* could remember, he had led the gentle *pescador* over the narrow blue-glazed bricks, past the wrought iron gate of the cathedral, and down the road to Condado. There, in the narrow mouth of the harbor, they kept a small, blue fishing boat.

In the summer they caught snapper and marlin and mackerel, and in the winter they caught lobster. The faithful *perro* and the gentle *pescador* shared the work, weathered together under the ocean sun, and journeyed home to share the same meal, the same fire, and to sleep side by side.

Each year, during those days when summer slips silently away, the sea would change, and the blue dancing waves become dark and stormy. The faithful *perro* dreaded these days for the gentle *pescador* was sure to say, "Mi *perrito fiel*, I must go alone today. The sea is not happy. *Huracán* is on his way. You must wait here for me today, where you will be safe."

The gentle *pescador* eyed the angry sea. His little boat tossed help-lessly while the faithful *perro* cried plaintively.

"Don't worry, *mi perrito fiel*! I shan't be long. The fish will jump in my nets, and soon I'll be home and we'll set ourselves safe for the night."

As the gentle *pescador* rowed farther and farther out to sea, the faith-ful *perro* whined and howled horribly.

"Stay, I shan't be long! Stay! Don't be afraid. . . ." At last the faith-ful *perro* could no longer hear the gentle *pescador's* good-byes.

To this day you will hear islanders say, "*Hasta hoy se queda mirando al mar y esperando*. . . ." It means, "Until today he stays, looking out to sea, waiting. . . ." They will take you to the place where the faithful *perro* waits, no longer afraid, but like a great rock, strong in his faithfulness.

130

Mi perrito fiel: My faithful little dog.

Huracán: hurricane

In Old San Juan, near the bridge to Condado, and not far from the San Geronimo fort, there is a famous coral shaped like a dog by the edge of the sea.

ALL THE WORLD'S BEAR

(WHO ELSE BUT POOH?)

Poem collected with the kind help of Marianna Meshkova

(1) AFRIKAANS, ARMENIAN, BRETON, BRAILLE, BULGARIAN, CHINESE, CROATIAN, CATALAN, CASTILIAN, CZECH,

DUTCH, ESPERANTO, FRENCH, FRISIAN, FAROESE, FINNISH, GERMAN, GREEK, GEORGIAN, HUNGARIAN, HE-

BREW, ITALIAN, JAPANESE, LATVIAN, LATIN, MACEDONIAN, MOLDOVIAN, POLISH, PORTUGUESE, ROMANIAN,

RUSSIAN, SLOVAK, SPANISH, SWEDISH, SIGN LANGUAGE, TATAR, TADJIK, THAI, UKRAINIAN, YIDDISH...

(2) Хорошо живёт
на свете
Винни-Пух!

Весело поёт
он эти песни
вслух!

И трещалки и
пыхтелки
и сопелки

И свистелки
«Тра-та-та!»

В голове моей
опилки....
не беда!

131

1. FORTY OF THE LANGUAGES WHICH WINNIE-THE-POOH KNOWS.*
2. POOH SONG IN RUSSIAN.
3. POOH SONG IN ENGLISH.
4. BEE HAVING THISTLE TEA.
5. POOH LOOKING PUZZLED.
6. THISTLE REPAIR KIT:
   - THISTLE TRIMMERS
   - THISTLE PAINTBRUSH
   - THISTLE SEED CATCHER
   - THISTLE GLUE
7. SHEDDING THISTLE.
8. ANOTHER WAY OF SAYING "A BEAR OF VERY LITTLE BRAIN".

(3) *Ah, for Winnie-Pooh what a life!*
Merrily he sings with all his might!
Tra-ta-ta he whistles and pipes,
Tra-ta-ta he snorts and puffs,
My head is full of sawdust,
but so what!

*We found forty, but we are quite sure there are many more.

The original English Winnie-the-Pooh was written by A.A. Milne and first published in London in 1926.

"Grandfather," asked Mishka,
"Is it just a story, or is it really true?"

BEAR HEART

by Nikolai Arjannikov

NCE there lived a young bear in a land where the earth was often covered with snow, and the nights were long and cold. It made no difference to the little bear, for he spent all his time reading. Most of all, he loved to read aloud. One day, while his grandfather sat listening, Mishka read a story about a world where huge, beautiful flowers grew, and where bright, colorful butterflies filled the sky.

Over and over he read the story aloud until he almost knew it by heart. "Grandfather!" asked Mishka excitedly, "Is it just a story, or is it really true?" Grandfather knew exactly what Mishka was thinking. "It's true, Mishka" he reluctantly replied. "But that world is far, far away and so hard to find!"

Grandfather scratched his side . . . and then his head, and finally said, "Ah, my Mishka, but still you are determined to go!" Grandfather could not help but know the feeling, for even he had often wondered what it would be like to smell a flower. Still, reading about a wonderful world was *not* the same as walking the long road to find it. And Mishka was not only young and small, but he wore glasses, without which he could not see much past the ends of his knees. Yet, there was nothing for Grandfather to do, but to do his best to prepare him. First, he found a small vine and tied it to either side of Mishka's glasses so he wouldn't lose them. Then he made him new overshoes and lined them with bits of pine straw fluff to make them thick and soft. Finally, if he should lose his way and become afraid, Grandfather gave him a new blue bell. "It will tell me where you are my little Mishka!" When Mishka heard it ring, he felt even more confident then before—quite sure he would be there in no time at all!

At last, Mishka said good-bye. On and on he walked, almost as confident as when he could still see Grandfather waving—until, that is, he came upon a strange, shaggy creature lying on the ground, crying. "Who are you sad beast," said Mishka shyly, "and why are you crying?"

"I'm a bison and I'm *very hungry* for I can't find anything to eat!"

"How sad," said Mishka comfortingly. "Why don't I give you my glasses? I don't really know where to go with them on, and so with them off it won't be too great a loss." With that, Mishka took off his glasses and tied them on the little bison's head. Then he patted his nose and started off again down the long road.

On and on and on he walked until one day he met a little wolf who was making a *horrible noise*. "Why are you making that noise?" cried Mishka.

"I'm howling," howled the little wolf, "because I stepped on a thorn and my foot is sore!"

"Don't howl, Boluchka!" said Mishka as convincingly as he could. "You

134

The bison originated in Eurasia and is one of the few members of the Bovidae, or cattle family, to have crossed the land bridge called the Bering Strait to North America in prehistoric times.

Boluchra: Little Wolf.

can have my new soft boots. I don't really know where I'm going on with them on, and so with them off, it can't be that much longer!" Mishka carefully pulled the thorn out of the little wolf's paw and then pulled both of his boots over the sore spot. With all his heart the little wolf thanked Mishka and the two parted.

Mishka picked up his new blue bell and rang it once just to cheer himself up. On and on and on he walked until one day he saw another creature, brown and white, with huge tears falling from her eyes. "Ah! Who are you," he called out in dismay, "and why are you so sad?" A little fawn looked up and replied, "I can't find my mother and she can't find me!"

"Don't cry, Oleanuchka! I'll give you my bell!" The little fawn smiled when she heard it ring. "Just you wait and see, it will bring your mother quickly!" Mishka patted her nose and then set off again down the road.

Mishka now had none of the things his grandfather had given him: no glasses, no overshoes, no new blue bell. He walked along with his head bent low, and so, of course, he couldn't help but see his feet. "Well," he thought, "I do still have me." And so he kept going.

On and on and on he walked until suddenly his nose began to twitch just like Grandfather's did when something good was about to appear. And what do you think? Mishka looked up, and here and there and everywhere were *huge* flowers, so big that even he could see them clearly! And all the animals he'd met on his way were here together playing. When the animals saw him they were all amazed! "Mishka, how did you find your way?"

"How? How?" said a wise old owl sitting in a tree, watching everything. "If you have a huge heart, you will always be going on the right road!"

135

Oleanuchka: Little Fawn.

This story was recorded orally and came about in the way that so many stories have evolved and spread throughout the world. Although Nikolai was born and raised in the Urals, a mountainous land that joins Europe with Asia, this story is not native to either Eastern Europe or Asia. It is a retelling of a Native American story he heard and adapted, incorporating details from his own homeland. In just this way, many familiar stories, such as "Sleeping Beauty" and "Beauty and the Beast", have come to be universal stories whose message is familiar to all children.

THE JOURNEY HOME

The last journey is the most important one. On this journey you must finally come *home*.

Map of the World

Journey III

Wherever you go,
go with all your heart

CHINESE PROVERB

Mankind has long dreamed of traveling into space. A story written in the 17th century, tells of a flock of wild geese carrying a brave explorer to the moon in 11 days.

A VOICE FROM SPACE

by Dr. Rhea Seddon,
NASA Astronaut . . . and Mom

NCE UPON a space shuttle there rode a famous lady astronaut whose name was Mom. Besides training to fly on the space shuttle and do sophisticated scientific research, she also had a little son named Paul. He was eight years old when Mom made her second flight into space aboard the Space Shuttle Columbia.

His school applied for the very special opportunity to speak to the astronauts on Mom's flight using a ham radio. The class worked hard to learn how communications with the shuttle worked. They learned how to use the ham radio, how to speak into the microphone, and how to say "Over!" when they had finished talking. Each member of the third grade class had to prepare

The first human to finally travel into space was Russian cosmonaut, Yuri Gagarin in 1961. The first humans to land on the moon were astronauts, Neil Armstrong and Buzz Aldrin in 1969.

questions they wanted answered from space. Paul was really worried that Mom would embarrass him by treating him differently from the other students. He worked out a deal with Mom that she would treat him just like any other student.

The Shuttle Columbia launched successfully and a few days later it was time for Paul's class to contact Mom and ask all their questions as the space shuttle flew across the United States. (That only takes nine minutes so everyone had to speak VERY QUICKLY!)

Finally it was Paul's turn. And just as they had planned, he asked his question and Mom answered just as she did for the other children. Then it came time to close the interview. Mom said to the class, "Thank you for calling! Your questions were great and I was happy to talk to you. Over!"

"Good-bye," said their teacher. And then, a little voice came over the radio (almost in a whisper) and said, "I love you, Mom. Have a safe trip home."

These are the special things that astronauts, and moms, hold in their hearts forever.

ONE THOUSAND PAPER CRANES

a Japanese legend

There
is a Japanese legend which
says ✣ If you fold *1000* paper cranes
the last one will fly away. In its heart your
wish will live and be given life. A little girl, be-
lieving what she was told, began to fold and fold.
Her name was Sadako. Her home was Hiroshima.
Her hope was for peace. She folded and folded. Then
other children helped too, for they also knew. ✣ There
are, to all appearances, terrible defeats in this world of
peace and freedom. Still, like the crane who opens
her wings to soar on the breeze she cannot see,
those who persist are not deceived. They
open their hearts and fly on all that
they quietly feel deep
inside.

Sadako was a child when the atomic bomb was dropped in 1945. Today a golden crane commemorates the children who perished. Under the bird are the words the children asked her to carry to the world: "This is our cry, this is our prayer, Peace in the world."

PETER FERBER

*Mei Ying wandered slowly down the road until she finally reached
the bamboo and rattan furniture shop of her Uncle Shi Lung.*

梅璞

MEI YING

143

by Jasmine Tsang

"WHAT CAN I DO now, M-ma?" Mei Ying asked her mother.

M-ma: mother.

It was August. It was very hot in Shanghai. School had been over for more than a month and Mei Ying was bored.

"Did you practice your calligraphy today?" M-ma asked straightening out the futon and pulling up the soft, silk cotton quilt. "You know, if you are diligent, beautiful characters will flow from your brush, as if all by themselves!"

futon: bedding.

Mei Ying sighed. "That's the *only* thing I did yesterday," she said wiping the perspiration from her face. "It takes too much effort, M-ma, in this hot, muggy weather! I promise I'll practice tonight."

She turned to walk away.

Understanding Mei Ying's frustration with the heat, M-ma called out *my little heart and liver: a very affectionate term, said in the same way as someone in the West might say, "my pet."*

Shi Lung means Shining Dragon.

144

feng zheng: kite.

to her tenderly, "Where are you going now my little heart and liver?"

"I don't know, M-ma. Maybe I'll go down to Uncle Shi Lung's shop."

Once more Mei Ying sighed and wiped the hot, beaded drops of water from her face and nose.

"People feel hotter, Mei Ying, when they are impatient!"

Mei Ying walked along the crowded, bustling streets, past the fabric stores and fish market, and the stall where the barber was busily at work cutting someone's hair. The merchants and pedicabs were making their way wearily through the August heat.

Mei Ying remembered her excitement when school was over in June. The weather was cooler then and there were gusty winds and heavy rains that fell in torrents. The wind tossed her hair and pulled her colorful *feng zheng* so swiftly that she felt as if she would suddenly go flying off with it! Watching her beautiful *feng zheng* soar before a storm was great fun.

There were always many children and families eager to test their kites before a storm—*chieh chiehs* (older sisters) and *mei meis* (younger sisters), *ko kos* (older brothers) and *dee dees* (younger brothers) each eager to take a turn. Sometimes the older children brought kites with lines strengthened by powdered glass and resin. They would chase the younger children's kites, using theirs like flying swords to cut the strings of weaker kites. It was always disappointing when Mei Ying's string was cut and her kite came fluttering to the ground.

Mei Ying loved to watch the flying kites—and was always one of the fastest to chase after any kite that tumbled. She spent hours tearing off the old worn paper from their frames and pasting on new brightly colored tissues. Then the kites were as good as new and ready to fly again.

On some June nights a gong would announce the monkey show. Of course, everyone, young and old, would throng toward it and form a large circle. Chanting loudly and beating his gong, the trainer would call out his commands. On cue, the monkey would go to a small box and take out an exotic mask! Wearing the face of the warrior hero *Quan Kong*, the monkey would strut about making threatening gestures. But when he wore the mask of the famous ancient beauty *Yang Quay Fay*, he mimicked the delicate mincing steps of a lady with bound feet. Sometimes, he put on the mask of the kitchen god and swaggered around the circle wagging his finger at the ladies while the trainer ranted about wastefulness, or cleanliness in the kitchen!

145

Mei Ying always laughed and cheered when she saw the monkey tottering like an old man, or juggling golden balls while wearing the mask of a clown—clapping her hands and stamping her feet in excitement.

After a few impersonations, the monkey would jump on the shoulder of his trainer and refuse to perform. The trainer and the monkey would carry on a lively argument until the man at last gave in and passed a hat for money. Sometimes Mei Ying would toss in the *yuan* she had been given that week for her allowance.

yuan: the dollar of China.

Then came July and the soft, dreamy days of constant rain. It was the same every July in Shanghai. Even so, there were interesting things to do. That was the time for paper folding games. Mei Ying knew how to make boats and all kinds of animals from sheets of colored paper.

When the sun came out, the paper boats were sent floating down open gullies and puddles in the street. Sometimes the boats were brought to the East Flower River, where Mei Ying often swam or helped her friends build little docks along the banks.

146

But now it was August in Shanghai—and hot. Everything was still and heavy. The Yangtze flowed without a ripple. Not a leaf stirred. The air hung over everything like a wet towel. The older children still went fishing in the murky August river, but Mei Ying was not welcome to tag along. They said she was too noisy.

Mei Ying wandered slowly down the road until she finally reached the bamboo and rattan furniture shop of her Uncle Shi Lung. He was sitting outside fanning himself, trying not to move, and drinking a soda.

"Hello, Mei Ying, Have you eaten your rice today?"

"Yes, Uncle Shi Lung, I am fine but, tell me, what can I do now that it is August?"

"When it is this hot, Mei Ying, the best thing to do is to sit and do nothing! That's what my customers do. I haven't seen one all day." Uncle Shi Lung rose to get Mei Ying a bottle of soda.

Mei Ying eagerly drew a quick gulp—and, suddenly, the bottle made a sound! She did the same thing again and, it was no mistake, the bottle made a sound! When Mei Ying blew air over it, it said "Whoo-oo," in a high voice. Then, when she sucked in her breath, the bottle replied "Sooo-oo." Suddenly, Mei Ying had forgotten all about her boredom and the heat.

"Whoo-oo . . . Sooo-oo . . . Whoo-soo," blew Mei Ying rhythmically.

147

After a few more sips, Mei Ying again blew over the now half-empty bottle and it said, "Whoo-oo," in a much lower voice! Then Mei Ying borrowed Uncle Shi Lung's empty bottle. Uncle Shi Lung's bottle had the lowest voice of all! Mei Ying smiled broadly. She had just discovered how to make bottles talk! Mei Ying was excited to have made such a great discovery even on a hot day.

She quickly bid her uncle good day and raced down to the corner food stand. It was where you could buy soda and fried cookies. There were also tempting pieces of candied ginger, dried orange peel, and jars full of watermelon seeds—some were salty and others milky sweet. But at that moment Mei Ying was not interested in any of these. The corner store was where the neighborhood children gathered and she was hoping to find her cousin Dar Dee and his friends Bar Shing and Ah Tau.

Dar Dee means Big Younger Brother.

Bar Shing means Eight Stars.

Ah Tau means Head.

As soon as Mei Ying spotted them she shouted, "Listen to this!" She then set up her bottles and showed them what she had discovered.

Dar Dee's face brightened. He found an empty wide-mouthed bottle and made the biggest sound of all. Soon the children were collecting bottles from here and there, and happily discovering the sound of each one's voice. The full bottles called out in high, shrill voices, and the big, empty ones answered with smooth, deep replies.

Then Bar Shing and Ah Tau began beating on the bottles with chopsticks. "Listen! The chopsticks have voices too!"

Soon, more and more children appeared, lining up bottles of different shapes and sizes—some full of water and others not so full. As the children blew and beat on their bottles, people came and stood in a circle around them. It was just like the monkey show—only the people were cheering *them*, thought Mei Ying!

Uncle Shi Lung had closed his shop and followed the sound of the bottle band. There was no sense missing the chance to join a crowd of spectators. Smiling, he took off his dark blue cap and told Mei Ling that she should pass it among the spectators.

Ba-ba: father.

Nai Nai: grandmother.

That night, beaming with pride, Mei Ying told M-ma, Ba-ba, and Nai Nai about the performance, showing them the shiny *yuan* Uncle Shi Lung had given her.

"Was it not too much effort in this hot weather?" asked M-ma with a twinkle in her eyes. As her mother spoke, Mei Ying suddenly remembered her morning complaints.

"Well, I tried and tried and the right tones came all by themselves!" M-ma smiled.

When it was time to practice calligraphy, Mei Ying no longer felt the heavy demands of discipline. With the voices of the bottles still fresh in her mind, her brush took wings and flew rhythmically through the prescribed lines. Soon, well balanced and finely proportioned letters began to form a chorus on the pages before her!

Can you make the characters in Mei Ying's exercise book? First try tracing them.

山　山　山

This is the symbol for the word above.

友　友　友

This is the symbol for friend.

悅　悅　悅

This is the symbol for happy or pleased.

雨　雨

This is the symbol for rain. Can you see the raindrops?

鳶　鳶

This is the symbol for kite. Can you see the kite?

PETER FERBER

Young Tam sped up the ladder swift as a squirrel.

BIG TAM AND WEE TAM

by Pippa Stuart

EVERY SPRING Tam arrived from town to work for us in the country. He could turn his hand to anything —painting, plumbing, tree felling and planting, carpentry, looking on us with profound scorn as feckless incompetents.

feckless: weak, ineffective.

One May morning he arrived, not, as usual, alone, but with a very small boy who had the pallor of city dwellers—and a face too old, too worldly-wise for his young years.

"Here's my boy, wee Tam, come to help me," said Big Tam. "He'd better learn early that life's not all play. He's here for to work."

Wee Tam nodded at this grim ethic as if he knew only too well that life might be a lot of things, but it certainly was not all play.

He proved at once that he had not come to idle, darting instantly to obey when summoned by his father's commands, "Hurry Tam! What are

yon: that

throttle: a way to hurt someone.

152

you up to down there? Fetch me up yon pot of red paint. Don't take a week," adding the fearsome threat, "If you spill as much as one drop I'll throttle you!"

I watched nervously as young Tam sped up the ladder, swift as a squirrel, swinging over the gutter and from there slithering nimbly over the tiles and up to the chimney stack.

"Is Wee Tam quite safe?" I called up. Big Tam flung me down a look of contempt. "Do you think I didn't see to that! He's here to learn."

"But not on our roof!"

Big Tam ignored that remark.

At their brief lunch break when I asked the two Tams to share our meal, Big Tam said grandly, "Aye, if you'se share ours." Theirs was hunks of white bread spread very thinly with margarine and jam. While we ate what he called our "jeely pieces," I plucked up courage and asked if it would be possible to spare Wee Tam for half an hour . . . well, seeing his expression, perhaps for twenty minutes? We were taking the dog for a walk and his boy might like to see the countryside around us, I timidly explained.

mair: more

"Twenty minutes, no mair, then."

Wee Tam followed us with a glance back at his father who had better things to do than gallivant around the country.

As we went, Tam became more at ease with us but remained wary of our collie. "He's very friendly", we assured him.

dugs: dogs

"Dugs bite", said Tam. "You can't tell me anything about dugs."

"Ours is fond of children."

"All dugs bite", repeated Tam with clearly a voice of experience.

We led him to the places that, since childhood, we had looked on as enchanted, fairy ground: the owl's hollow tree, the birch woods where tame squirrels ate nuts from our hands, the lochan where the cob swan, his pen, and five cygnets glided among water lilies. The fields were gold with buttercups. From far off came the cuckoo's last call—the sign that spring was slipping into summer.

Tam who, until now, knew only city streets, had his first glimpse of a cow. He tried to hide his alarm. "WHAT'S YON?! . . . Ooo, so it's a coo. It's about as big as the bus that brought us here from town."

With that danger safely confronted, his self-confidence returned. He became eager to tell us about some of the neighbours of the tenement where he lived with his Ma and Pa, and three little sisters.

"They're a strange lot up our close", he said. "There's blind Uncle Barney. He's always falling doon the stairs. He'd be steadier if he only had his eyes back, he says. You should hear the yells and screeches he lets out. 'You pushed me!' That's what he tells old Tib. Old Tib's his enemy. 'I never pushed you! Tib rhymes with fib—you're a liar! You're a stranger to the truth,' Uncle Barney shouts back at him. Uncle Barney is always telling me and my wee sisters always to keep to the truth."

Once Wee Tam had begun, nothing would stop him and his tales of city life. "There's rats all around—big whiskery ones. Wild Patrick sets his big mastiff dug on them. My wee sisters go louping past Patrick, fast as fleas! They're scared of his hands, like claws they are, and of his great snarling dug—it's a terror."

lochan:
cob: male swan
pen: female swan
cygnets: baby swans

153

coo: cow

close: a narrow passage leading from the street to a courtyard.

doon: down

louping: running

Wee Tam stopped to draw breath, edging closer to us when a herd of Highland cattle—shaggy-coated, with enormous wide-spreading horns—charged down the meadow toward us.

"They're really very gentle for all their size", we reassured Tam.

"Aye, just like your dug", he answered unconvinced.

"We could visit the farm now", we suggested. "It's near milking time. You could see the cows being milked and the last litter of kittens. There's the hay loft where we used to make tunnels in the hay when we were your age. . . ." Tam wasn't even listening.

"It's time I was getting back to my faither. He needs me to help him."

As soon as we reached the garden gate Wee Tam set off at a run heading straight for the ladder and the rungs that led to the sloping roof and the chimneys and the pot of red paint.

I had begun to make plans and dream of having Tam to stay for a summer weekend that might turn into a week or even longer. He would be far from the crowded tenement, the whiskery rats, the "fechts" between blind Uncle Barney and spiteful Tib, the threats of Wild Patrick and his snarling mastiff. I saw Wee Tam growing taller, his pale cheeks becoming rosy country ones. He would get to know a quite different aspect of life. By the time we followed him through the gate, Tam was high on the roof ridge surveying his father's paintwork and calling, "Coming Pa, jist a jiffy!"

Towards five o'clock I infused a pot of tar-black tea Tam enjoyed when the day's work was ended. As we sat together on the lawn I made my second request: Perhaps he would allow Wee Tam to come to us for a week-

154

faither: father

fechts: fights

jist: just

end, even a week, during the summer—if he could be spared, that was. He might be the better for the country air, and we would take the *greatest care* of him. My voice trailed away.

Tam sat there stolidly, cup in hand, silent. Had I offended him? Had I given the impression that I knew better than he did how to bring up a child? He took another slurp of tea, fixing me with his steady gaze. At last he spoke.

155

"It would be better if you asked the boy himself."

"Well then, Tam," I started again, "what do you think? Would you like to see the room you'd have if you came?"

Tam looked up from munching a slice of fruit cake.

"I'll be having to pack my faither's tools", was all the answer he gave.

He gathered them together with enormous care, stowing them away in a canvas bag. Nothing more was said about my invitation. It was as if I had not uttered a word.

They set off down the country lane, young Tam swinging the canvas tool bag and whistling. *Far too heavy* for a child, I thought with a kind of exasperation and strong sense of failure. Big Tam's deep voice came echoing back on the still air.

"Well you didn't say yes or no to the woman."

"Oh that!" said Wee Tam dismissing it with a shrug. "I don't want to bide there. It's far too quiet! The trees in that wood gave me the creeps, so did the big horned beasts. She says they mean no harm and she says their dug would never bite, but I bet it does, jist like Patrick's snarler—and when you're least expecting it! Anyway, I'd far raither be helping you."

bide: stay

raither: rather

They vanished off into the green twilight, Wee Tam skipping happily beside his father, no doubt proud of being able to deal with high ladders and even taller chimney stacks, sure-footed and unafraid.

In one day I had learned from father and son, Big Tam and Wee Tam, a lesson I was not likely to forget. I had made the mistake of planning to rescue someone who hadn't the slightest wish to be rescued; of playing the benefactor where none was wanted or needed.

THE POSTMAN

A Turkish children's rhyme
Collected and translated with the kind help of Diane Cihangir

postaci: postman

Postaci

Bak postaci geliyor	Soon the postman is due—
Selam veriyor	Everyday he comes saluting!
Herkes ona bakiyor	We can hardly wait to see
Merak ediyor	What he has for you and me!
Çok sevinçli haberler	Oh, here he comes at last!
Getirdin bize	And what happy news he has!
Çok teşekkür ederiz	Letters, postcards, parcels too
Postaci size	Oh, we sing our thanks to you!
Bügünlük bu kadar	That is all for today!
Hoşça kaliniz	We must say goodbye and wait
Yarin yine geliriz	We will come again tomorrow.
Unutmayiniz	Do not forget, do not be late!

The young man was singing
as if he was on a stage.

THE PERFORMANCE

A true story of a man named Kolya

PEOPLE WERE rushing here, there, and everywhere, thinking only of getting home and having something to eat! It was noisy in the metro. It was noisy on the street. It was even noisy on top of the buildings where pigeons sat complaining about all the commotion the people were making. Kolya was very hungry. For breakfast he had had two cups of tea. For lunch he had had two cups of tea. Yet, he was happy for there was money in his pocket that he had worked hard to earn all week. It wasn't that he didn't work hard every week. It was just that he wasn't always paid.

A *reenok* was not far away. If he hurried he still might find some nice bread and salad and meat. He had not gone far when he came to a stop. People pushed by him, no one seeing him; no one hearing. Yet Kolya had stopped for a young man was singing. He had never heard anything so beautiful or pleasing. Kolya listened on and on, for it seemed to him the performer was giving people a reason for living instead of just existing, and Kolya was grateful. He left reluctantly, but before he did, he reached into his pocket and gave the young blind man all the money he had made.

When Kolya got home he was singing. Misha, a neighbor, was waving at him. "Kolya, *zdrastvue!* How late you are tonight! You must be starving. Come quickly, my wife will make a plate for you."

This story took place in Moscow nearly ten years after the breakup of the Soviet Union. For most people life was still very difficult.

АВТОБУС: *a bus ticket costing two rubles.*

reenok: outdoor market.
zdrastvue!: greetings!

VALERIE SCHURER CHRISTLE

The mail fell into the front hall, which led to the front room, which
led to the kitchen, which led to the back door, which led to the garden.

It's quite easy, frankly, to give money to this good cause or that.
A generosity of spirit is far rarer.

TWO MORE CHILDREN AND
AN EXTRA ROW OF BEANS

A true story thanks to Jane Davies and her garden

SOME ROADS were made for taking you places; some for bringing you home, and others, like the narrow ones that wound through the small towns of England, held tidy brick houses in their places. On every front door in Dedham was a mail slot with a shiny brass flap to keep out the rain. Twice each day, you could hear the mail fluttering to the floor and the flap clattering back into place. The mail fell into the front hall, which led to the front room, which led to the kitchen, which led to the back door, which led to the garden.

Westgate House was no exception. Its back door was blue and led you to the garden where apple trees stood like nannies chatting and laughing, and all the while keeping a careful eye on the color of the peas, the height of the beans, the ripeness of the gooseberries—and Jane.

The road from Wivenhoe, or even Tenpenny Heath, will finally take you to Dedham, which, according to my map at least, is exactly one inch from Cattawade and two from either Tattingstone, or Goose Green, all of which are in Essex in the East of England, which floats serenely in the blue North Sea.

162

£12 is approximately $17 U.S. dollars.

In 1994, Jane's small garden earned about $1000 U.S. dollars. It is impossible to say exactly how many children an acre garden can keep but, over the years, Jane has succeeded in being more than a little needed.

Jane worked each day in the garden. You could tell by her hands. They were washed by the sun and tinted with the resin of the rich soil. In the spring she patted down seeds, in the summer plucked up weeds, and in the fall collected apples before the wind had a chance to claim them. Jane had dark brown hair and dark brown eyes, and the smile of one who spent her time tending to what is new and growing. Each day, she checked to see if anyone had bought something from the small wooden table that stood at the front of Westgate. On it was a carefully painted sign which read:

Fruits and Vegetables

A good day would bring £12, though some days she would sell nothing at all, which was always discouraging. If no one had come, she would move the table to the side, out of the sun, and then tidy up the lot of envelopes people used to send their money through the mail slot and on to the front hall floor. It was rare for money to be stolen. People often gave extra.

By November, it would be time for Jane to tally up the Garden Journal she kept each day. Soon would be the holidays. She would collect all she had made and take it to the bank where the clerk, recognizing her immediately, would say, "Well, well, Mrs. Davies where to this year?"

When he had made all his calculations he would give her a bank draft and wish her well. This year, like last, it would be sent to help orphans in Romania. She was quite sure there was enough to help twelve, two more than last year. Nonetheless, feeling a bit apologetic, on her way out you could always hear her say, "It's a pity it's not a bit more. Still, it's quite lovely, really, to be even a little needed."

Journal

Each product raised as follows:

. . . .	gooseberries	. . . .	£ 36
. . . . .	white currants	. . . .	£ 26
. . . . .	blackc.	. . . .	£ 45
. . . .	blackberries	. . . .	£ 28
. . . . . .	runner beans	. . . .	£ 62.50
. . . . . .	strawberries & raspberries	. . . . .	£ 10
. . . .	damsons	. . . .	£ 4.50
. . . . . .	apples	. . . .	£ 80 (!)
. . . . . .	tomatoes	. . . .	£ 7.50

Bulbs sold in small packets at £1 each:

. . . .	bluebells	. . . .	£ 51
	snowdrops		£ 59
. . . .	daffodils	. . . .	£ 26
. . . .	grape hyacinths	. . . .	£ 17
. . . . .	aconite corms	. . . .	£ 15
. . . . . .	bundles of iris berries	. . . .	£ 9

Plants 50p to £3 depending on size:

| | Total plants sold | . . . . . £150 |
| | Misc. sales | . . . . . £ 83.50 |

| | Grand total | . . . . . £710 |

discovered wild strawberry
this year!

Note: most sold at £1.50
(mostly to a friend)

very satisfactory —

Notes

This year more plants and bulbs added
Too bad, no plums or figs
Extra lot of blackc. & apples before other people had theirs
Put in an extra row of runner beans

first pansies 3/26

GOOSEBERRIES ⚜ WHITE CURRANTS ⚜ BLACKCURRANTS ⚜ BLACKBERRIES ⚜ RUNNER BEANS ⚜ STRAWBERRIES & RASPBERRIES ⚜ DAMSONS ⚜ APPLES ⚜ TOMATOES ⚜ SNOWDROPS ⚜ BLUE

GOOSEBERRIES ⚜ WHITE CURRANTS ⚜ BLACKCURRANTS ⚜ BLACKBERRIES ⚜ RUNNER BEANS ⚜ STRAWBERRIES & RASPBERRIES ⚜ DAMSONS ⚜ APPLES ⚜ TOMATOES ⚜ SNOWDROPS ⚜ BLUE

THE PEOPLE THEY DID SING

A true story of the people of Mozambique

THE PEOPLE they have a spirit. They don't have things, so they have a spirit. The people they were planting their seeds, they were working, they were growing copra and cotton, cassava and tea. It was the rainy season. The wind, oh, she was angry! Her name it was Eilene. She wore a big, black dress, and when she cry, oh, how it bring down the rain!

The big river, the Limpopo, she broke her banks. She was catching the rain. She can catch no more. So she break. She cannot wait for the day. The sun he was sleeping—but the big river she cannot wait. She break. And so the land it is no more. The precious crops they are no more. The useful road, it is no more.

The people they leave their homes. Quickly! Quickly! They climb the trees. They bring beloved children to the top of the trees. They bring beloved grannies to the top of the trees. They bring their chickens and goats, and all their hopes. All day they wait. The night it is coming. The children they are crying. They are wet and hungry. They are afraid. The goats and chickens they are afraid. The night it is coming. The mamas and papas they are afraid. The wind, oh, she is raging. But one, she is not afraid! She is Old Grandmommie. Her name is Simiao. She look up at Eilene and she start to SING! And the people they are listening. They are hearing old Simiao sing. They are not hearing Eilene.

165

Simiao she is singing, she is making her prayers, and the people they are listening. When she stops—someone else he is beginning. He sings, and when he stops, someone else she is beginning. The children they are not afraid. The goats and the chickens they are not afraid. The mamas and the papas they are not afraid, for the people they sing. All through the night, the people they sing. The next day come and the people they sing. The people they sing for eight nights, songs—'til nine days gone, and the people they sing! The people they are waiting in the arms of the trees —in the arms of the trees and in the arms of hope! It is holding up the branches, it is holding up the children, it is holding up the goats! The people they are waiting in the arms of hope.

The people they wait. The sun it comes—and the water it goes. The people they are starting—they are building their homes, they are sowing their seeds, they are making their roads. And the people they sing.

This true story of the people singing to each other occurred in February of 2000 when floods swept through most of Mozambique. The Limpopo broke her banks at 4 a.m. one morning. Within an hour the waters completely covered the land.

*Little glowworms, sparkling, came out to show the children the way
until there, at the top of a hill, stood a tree whose silvery trunk gleamed
mysteriously from top to bottom.*

THE SILVERY TREE

by Marion Habicht

Translation from the original German by Marion Habicht

NOT VERY long ago, there was a time of great war, when countries were ruined and families broken apart: parents from their children and children from their mothers and fathers. The survivors of this war fled to regions where no battles disturbed the earth, and where fields and forests, not burdened with day to day cares, were calling for peace.

So it was that one day, as the light was falling short, four children left, walking hand in hand over the fields, toward the deep forest. All around them tall stalks of corn, full of fruit, lulled themselves to sleep in the light breath of the evening breeze. This was not, however, where the children could rest. They walked until night had fallen and the green hills above the river were covered by blankets of darkness. The deep, dark forest lay before them now and filled them with fear. Still they walked on as they

This story was written during the height of the war in Bosnia in 1994 when thousands of refugees were flooding over the mountains into Austria and other surrounding countries.

had been firmly told by the people of the town, "Do not stop until you find the silvery tree and there you will find peace!" This is what the people of the town had told the children when it fell to ruins.

The night was dark and gloomy. There was yet no moon nor comforting stars. "Do not cry! Make no sounds," the old people had sternly warned them! "When you are crying the grass will also cry, as well as the leaves of the willow. The ground will tremble and threaten to devour you if you cry! Therefore, no matter what, do not cry—make no sound! Hold fast your galloping heart and remain silent. Put wild mint in your hair in order to banish the will-o-wisps who will whisper to you to turn back to the fields and the moor."

The children remembered the warning of the old people. They gathered closer together. They watched that not one of them got lost. They found comfort in thinking of the silvery tree waiting to give them warmth and security. And they walked on.

Gently and steadily a brightness spread through the night as millions of brilliant stars filled the sky. The forest became brighter and the gloom vanished. Little glowworms, sparkling, came out to show the children the way through the thicket and swamp, until there, at the top of a hill, stood a tree whose silvery trunk gleamed mysteriously from top to bottom.

"Oh, there is the tree, the place we were meant to find our new home!" thought the children excitedly. And all around them the soft voices of the swaying grass encouraged them to go farther until they reached the mysterious shining tree. Over the silvery tree the crescent moon was shining like a great shelter. Her gentle light laid a blue-glimmering veil over the forest and the heads of the children as they lay beneath the tree on the soft moss to sleep for the night. Quietly, the forest animals crept up beside them, breathing their warmth and guarding the children's slumber. The owl watched above them, while fox and deer, hedgehogs and hares, and squirrels and frogs murmured their low blessing around them, "Sleep well, little children, sleep well. You are safe, little children, you are safe!"

169

Beneath the light of the silvery tree everyone was free from fear and full of peace. The fox did not care to hunt the hare nor the squirrel; the owl let the mice and frogs be. And the stars faithfully kept watch through the night until the morning star appeared: a new day's light was drawing near.

As the glowing copper sun sparkled and rose, the children stirred and opened their eyes. And there beneath them, in the young morning light, lay a village in the valley.

"We are waiting for you," called out the rooftops shining in the morning light.

"We are waiting for you," called out the gentle morning mist.

"We are waiting for you," called out the kindly people. "You are home!"

In the luminous rays of a perfectly dawned new day, the children ran to the village—their laughter and rejoicing reaching up to the heavens.

It was like seeing a new world,
made up of everyone of all different colours living together in harmony.

RAINBOWS

by Ann Kenrick

THEY WERE only three years old, they were only in Nursery School, and they had only just learned to blow soap bubbles. Frankie had dark hair, twinkling brown eyes, and a dark skin. He had come with his family from Africa to live in London, England. Tommy had fair hair, laughing blue eyes, and a light skin, and he was English. Neither Tommy nor Frankie had yet learned the secret of the rainbow, however.

Do you know the secret of the rainbow?

They appear during a storm when the sun suddenly breaks through the clouds even though it's still raining. That's no secret! When the sun fills the drops of rain a beautiful arch of light appears. It looks like an arch of colour because that's what light is—seven different colours: red, orange, yellow, green, blue, indigo and violet, all blended together. It takes light passing through the raindrops and then reflected on them in a special way to see the colours.

But that's not the *secret* of the rainbow either. Still, you have to look carefully to see all the colours because they blend together so perfectly.

Rainbows can appear almost anywhere—during a storm, at the edge of a waterfall, in a garden fountain, or even in a soap bubble. It was in a soap bubble that Frankie and Tommy saw their first rainbow—and then discovered the secret. It happened like this.

172

One day when playschool was over, while the children were all excitedly putting on their coats and waiting for their mothers to collect them, for no reason at all Frankie took out his fist and clipped Tommy round the ear. Tommy, of course, began to cry, for no matter how old you are it's never nice to be clipped round the ear. When Tommy's mum came to collect him he told her through his tears what Frankie had done.

He waited for his mum to scold Frankie . . . ! But she didn't. Then he waited for her to complain to the teacher. But she didn't do that either! Instead, very quietly, she said to him, "You know, Tommy, Frankie really wants to be your friend but he doesn't quite know how to tell you that."

Tommy was so surprised he didn't know what to say!

The next day at Nursery School when all the children were playing together, Frankie tried to hit Tommy again. This time Tommy ducked! That wasn't all he did though. This time Tommy went up to Frankie and put his arm around Frankie's shoulder. Then in a big, strong voice he said, "Frankie! You're my friend and friends don't hit each other!" That was the day Frankie and Tommy decided to blow bubbles together now that they were friends.

Frankie had made a champion size bubble when suddenly a little rainbow magically appeared on the bubble's surface. "Look!" yelled Frankie. Tommy stared a long time at the beautiful multi-coloured bubble and then looked again at Frankie. Frankie looked at all the different colours, too, and then at Tommy. Then they smiled at each other. They knew. They just knew the secret of the rainbow.

At that moment their teacher appeared. "Ah, a rainbow has found you has it?" she said cheerfully. "And do you know why you love looking at it?" she asked quietly.

173

Frankie and Tommy nodded. After that they were inseparable, almost like a walking rainbow.

A man born in Africa, like Frankie, a man named Desmond Tutu, had a vision once about the secret of the rainbow. For a long, long time the people of his country had been taught to be afraid of people from different backgrounds, or whose skin colour was not the same as their own. For over forty years his homeland, South Africa, had man-made laws that kept black people and white people always apart from one another. It was called *apartheid*. There were restaurants for black people and other restaurants for white people. White families lived in certain parts of the country and black families in other parts. Black children and white children went to separate schools so they never learned to play with each other. Even the huge beautiful beaches around Cape Town were restricted to black areas and white areas.

174

Quoted from Desmond Tutu's book, The Rainbow People of God *(NY, Doubleday, 1994), p256.*

Eventually, the separation caused fear, hatred, and violence among the people. There were, however, many people—teachers and ministers, as well as ordinary people and a few brave politicians—who understood that this wasn't the way their country was meant to be—and they began to work and pray to change it. In his vision, Desmond Tutu saw a very different world from the one his eyes could see. There was still the earth and light, but the light was different from sunlight. In his vision the light was a promise. Instead of being made up of different coloured rays, it was made up of all the people of his country. He saw people of different colours all living happily together as brothers and sisters. We are "the rainbow people of God," he said. "We have been made for togetherness. . . ."

Are you wondering how people can be a rainbow? Well, we *are* a rainbow and I will tell you how!

After forty long years, apartheid was finally brought to an end. That was in 1991. Then, in 1994, something very special happened. For the first time in their lives black people were allowed to vote. A very brave man, named Nelson Mandela, who had worked all his life to help end apartheid, was elected president. He urged people to forgive one another and to work to understand each other.

I was visiting a friend in Cape Town soon after Mr. Mandela became president. South Africa is at the southernmost tip of the African continent and Cape Town is in the southernmost part of South Africa, surrounded by beautiful beaches. The last day I was with my friend it was a public holiday. It was a very hot summer's day and so everyone had headed down to the beach to swim and play. My friend and I started off to the beach we had always gone to, the one that had once been designated for white people. Soon we could see the grassy bank that lines the beach. We could hear the ocean crashing on the shore and the sounds of people's voices. All the while we imagined the feel of the cold, salty waves tumbling over our feet and ankles as the sun beat down on our heads and on our backs!

175

Then, at last, we saw the brilliant blue ocean glistening and sparkling in the bright noon daylight. And there, all along the beach, were little children and big children, mothers and fathers, strangers and friends, white and black and every other color, all laughing and singing and playing *together*. For the first time in their lives, white children were playing football with black and Indian children, while their parents played softball and cricket—all like one large, happy family. Of course everyone was dipping in and out of the playful waves, swimming, surfing, shouting and singing! Do you know what it felt like? A new world. It was bright and full of the light that Desmond Tutu and so many others had dreamed of. It was made up of everyone of all different colours living together in harmony.

Did everyone see the rainbow I saw that day? Many did, I'm sure, but probably not everyone. That's part of the secret of the rainbow. Just as the light has to pass through the raindrops in a special way to make the rainbow appear, unless we look at our world in a new way, with a new kind of love filling our hearts, we won't see what's really there.

That evening my friend took me back to the airport to catch the big South African jumbo jet that would take me back to London. I knew it would be big—but I could hardly believe my eyes when I looked and saw that from the nose of the plane to the tip of its tail it was painted in all the colours of the rainbow!

It was getting dark by the time the plane was to take off. The stars were beginning to twinkle in the indigo sky. If there had not been a pane of glass in the way, I would have reached out and snatched a star to carry back with me to London!

176

Journey I

The name of the Mountain is Nobility. It is not a place you will find on a map, but a way to live, and so you will find this Mountain within. The higher you climb on this Mountain, the more you will see the world as it was really meant to be.

Journey II

The great secret that belongs to animals is innocence. It is what makes them free from prejudice, intolerance, or hate—things which we are *not* born with, but which we are taught. These are the things we must not learn.

Journey III

If you could travel to outer space, it would be easy to see that there are no borders dividing us into countries and places where only certain people are allowed to be. The secret of the journey home is that our home is not just a small town or even a large country, but a whole world.

Index

179

The beautiful little wooden animals that appear on pages 90 and 91, were carved by a Ghanaian artist. They passed through many hands before being purchased at an art fair sponsored to support African artists. Sadly, we do not know the artist's name, nonetheless we wanted to honor and share even a little of the beauty of Ghanaian art with you.

OUR FAVORITE STORY

To GET SOMETHING OUT OF A BOOK, you have to put a lot into it. First, we had to find authors and artists who lived in far away places (even outer space!). We wrote letters, sent faxes and zapped e-mails. But most often, we called friends . . . who called friends . . . who called more friends. Some were teachers, others were journalists, Peace Corp workers, translators, authors, artists, musicians, museum curators, and librarians. Soon, people were calling us back from Iceland and Australia, and the post office in Strathmiglo, Scotland. Finally the day came when we had found all the stories you've read in this book.

Should you ever be in India or Iceland, or Strathmiglo, Scotland, and come across one of the following people, know that you're meeting some-one very special. In addition to all the people whose names appear in this book, the other kind people who helped make it possible were: Postmaster, Strathmiglo, Scotland, Lui Collins, Julia Cuniberti, Nancy Currier, Eleanor Drummond, Naomi Greeland, Nausicaa M. Habimana, R. E. Hughes, Tracy Jay, Amy Louis, Jill and John Maneschi, Robert Marquand, Patti and Grover Moore, Doug Peterson, K. Ragnheinur, Lise Richardson, Jo Seagren, Lori Robinson, Susan and Kurt Stark, Kristin Steinsdottir, Mr. and Mrs. Gerald VanTilborg, B.T. Tochiev, Wolfeboro Public Library staff, Elizabeth Ziegler, and Elmer's Glue-All.

Our sincerest thanks.

Andover Green Book Publishers

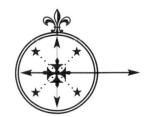

Don't you agree, a book is a good place to meet? Do come again, and bring a friend if you'd like.

And now before you leave, don't forget to take your favorite story. I intended it for you to keep.

With love,
Mrs. Figle